YOU KNEW THE PRICE

NOTHING IS PROMISED 2

SUSAN KAYE QUINN

———

The choice you make is the future you create.

Climate-driven plagues haunt humanity, and it's Regional Director Zuri Hill-Gray's job to keep the clean-energy grid running.

Zuri has the perfect life—a beautiful home on the Hillstead, a loving family, and a powerful job keeping the LA Basin's grid humming. If only she didn't see the ghost of her dead twin in the mirror. Her grief-counselor husband understands too much, her Aunties Cora and Vivian smother her to excess, and her mother can't look at her daughter without seeing the half that's missing.

Zuri can't begin to face her sister's little daughter—to Ruby, Zuri is the ghost.

Which is why she's running away to work, again, on the anniversary of her sister's death.

Then a power engineer walks into Zuri's office and claims someone is stealing energy from Power Island One—and they've tried to kill her to cover it up. The more Zuri digs, the more it's clear someone's been tinkering in the shut-down fusion labs. They're going to dangerous lengths to hide it, and it's been happening right under her nose. Which is how Regional Directors lose their jobs.

Zuri's already lost her better half—she can't afford to lose this, too.

You Knew the Price is the second of four tightly-connected hopepunk novels in a near-future climate-fiction series. It's about our future, how society lives on invisible things, like electricity and trust, that are far too easy to break... and how our most difficult moments are often when we discover the only path forward is healing not just ourselves but the world.

ONE

ZURI LOST TIME WHEN SHE TALKED TO GHOSTS.

Her twin sister gazed at her from her reflection in the window. The deep brown of Zuri's skin became darker still in the glass, the morning sun not reaching the phantom of Amani trapped inside. Beyond the window, light skittered across the hillside's scrub brush, tumbled down Topanga's Canyon, then skipped across the sparkling waters of the Pacific Ocean to land on the low hills of Catalina Island.

Farther still, beyond the horizon, lay the Power Islands. *Her work.*

"That's all I do," Zuri confessed to her ghostly reflection. She and Amani had always spoken over each other, sharing sentences, but now there was only the Zuri-half. She'd let her hair grow out natural, and it was getting big—a dark halo as full and round as Amani had ever worn it. "I should cut it," Zuri whispered. Amani's lips barely moved, the ghost having her sister's dark, serious eyes, but none of the fire, none of that actor's *aliveness* that had always sparked within. All of it, gone. Now Amani could only judge Zuri with her own steely, dead expression.

"I know. I'm trying."

A shriek from outside her home office jolted Zuri so badly she had to grip the arms of the chair to keep from sliding out. It was just one of the kids—could be Jayden or Audre, they both had those high-pitched, ear-drum-puncturing yelps—but Zuri still had to tell her heart to settle. Sounded like someone was having fun, not dying. She wrenched her gaze away from the window and flicked a glance at the corner of her display, hovering in the air even closer than the reflection. *9 am.* She'd lost an hour. Worse than normal, but the date next to the time reminded her why.

One year. The kind of anniversary no one wants.

She'd scheduled a full day of work—reports and prep, mostly, but she also had an appointment at her office in LA... which she'd be late for, if she didn't get her butt moving. It felt like rolling a boulder up the canyon, but she hauled her body out of the chair. Then she gave herself two deep breaths and a glance at the window, but the angle was all wrong now—no reflection.

She shook her head, chastising her need to even look, and yet absently stretched one of her curls, checking the length. The end was frizzled. *Amani would take better care.* Zuri squeezed her eyes shut, let the curl go, opened her eyes again.

A message popped up in her peripheral vision, with the custom pulse that meant it was from her assistant, Jeevika. Zuri pulled in a breath and swiped it open.

What difference do it make if the thing you scared of is real or not? –Toni Morrison

Jeevika had a habit of sending quotes at the beginning of the day, a preamble to the onslaught of the day's work. Zuri used to reply with her own, trying to out-quip her assistant, but that habit had faded away. It took more energy than she possessed. Jeevika kept sending them, regardless, and she'd been on a Toni Morrison run for a while. Zuri didn't have the heart to tell her to stop. Jeevika was up in Toronto now, a climate migrant first from India and now escaping the heat of LA but still serving as her personal assistant, organizing her work and keeping her on track. Jeevika was probably the only thing keeping her afloat for the last year.

Zuri pulled up the rest of the message. *The Quarterly Reports for Power Islands Six through Twelve are in your folder in prep for next week's review meetings. I've pulled last week's grid management data for you, but that's still processing—I'll send it over when it's ready. That Santa Monica desalination project is still on hold, pending an environmental review, but the project manager keeps calling and demanding to speak with you. I'll hold them off as long as you like. And I know you never want to talk to the state regulators, but they are quite insistent they want to talk to you. It's about the Palm Springs solar farm protests. They're heating up, and there's chatter a major environmental group is joining. Not our region, but of course, Palm Springs is a major supplier to our grid. Oh, and I've set up that appointment with the intern in your office this morning, per your request. It's on your calendar. But everything else can really wait until Monday, Madam Director! Enjoy your weekend.*

Zuri sighed. Nothing could pierce the determined cheerfulness Jeevika carried with her like it was the only supply on earth. Zuri tried to tap some of that energy as she strode out of her office. Her family's house was small, like all the homes on the Hillstead, but it had plenty of room for two growing kids... and a husband who got right down and played with them.

The sight of them in the living room brought her up short, frozen at the edge of the hallway. *They were dancing.* Little Audre on her three-year-old legs mostly hopped. Her big brother Jayden's five-year-old moves had a bit more going on, but her husband was the king of that swing. Zuri couldn't hear the beat—they had the pocket sound on, the tech tracking their ears and enveloping them in sound only they could hear—but she could feel it in the big joyful energy of Denzel's arms swinging, his legs stepping, his whole body alive in that silent music of motion. He lifted his arms, shimmying his hands in the air—Audre and Jayden leaped to copy him. Then he brought it down low, his tall body folded in half, feet still tapping that beat, hands jazzing the floor. The kids did the same until he swept Audre up and circled her high. She let out that shriek Zuri had heard before, and the pure joy of it pierced her.

With a flick of her finger, she could tell her chip interface to activate the sound tracker. It would find her ears, surround them with sound, and she could join her family in their moment of dance-with-aban-don. Live and breathe and smile and gasp with delight again.

She stayed where she was.

She could sneak out without them seeing, if she left now, but guilt rooted her at the edge of the hall, indecision digging her a spot to stay. Denzel caught sight of her as he twirled Jayden next. He did a double-take, frowned, and in that instant, she was caught.

"Pocket sound, mute," he said, a little breathless from the dance. Then to Jayden, as he set him down, "You keep going. Keep going!" Denzel was already backing away, coming to see her. Jayden carried on, dancing some kind of gyration around his little sister's jackhammer moves, her tiny curl puffs shaking like crazy.

Denzel turned his approach into a saunter. His dead-sexy smile was too much.

But hers was reflexive in return. "Mr. Hill-Gray, you are one fine specimen." And he was—all tall, dark-skinned, and smooth-moving.

He reached her, his hands warm, sliding around her. "I was starting to think you'd forgot." He shaved his head these days but kept his beard trimmed neat. It was soft as he nuzzled up against her.

"The kids—"

"Let 'em dance." Then he kissed her, and Denzel never kissed with anything less than his entire being. His whole big, Black strong body. There was nothing else in the world when this man kissed, and it had stolen her heart from the very first time.

But now was different. The part of her that died with Amani was still gone.

She *tried*. But that was the thing with Denzel—husband, father, counselor; *grief counselor* who'd lost his own parents long ago—there was no fooling him.

Even when she was desperate to.

He pulled back, some of the sparkle still lingering in his eyes despite the slight frown. "I'll just tell these kids to dance the whole damn *Whozits* album, while I take you upstairs a little while—"

"Denzel, no."

His frown deepened, so she let her hands apologize, flat on his chest. "I *want* to, I just..." Then she couldn't put any more words into it, simply shook her head instead.

He leaned a little away, giving her space but not letting go. "It's been a year, Z."

"I know it." Was he just acknowledging the date or saying she should be over it? *No,* that was her own head. Denzel would say no such thing. "I'm just not there yet."

"I know." And he did—she could see it in his eyes, the infinite depth of understanding, and that was also too much. Her guilt tripled down, saying she didn't deserve this man.

She hugged him, half apology, half desperate banishing of that stupid voice in her head. She *did* deserve this. All of this. Something was simply broken in her, and it kept her from holding it as close and fierce as she was holding her husband.

He held her, just as long as she wanted.

When she pulled back, the choking feeling had been beaten down. "I have to get going."

"Into the office? Today?" His eyebrows lifted. "It's Saturday."

Was it? Somehow that had escaped her. Part of her had contrived to be busy this day, this anniversary day, but had somehow suppressed that it was the weekend. *Family time.* That used to mean Amani and her family—Marcel and little Ruby—not to mention the rest of the Hillstead, but over the last year, the weekends had slowly telescoped down to just Denzel and the kids... when she allowed it at all.

"I... have someone I have to meet. Face-to-face. Personnel problem." Which was true, although she could have let someone in the office handle this intern's problems, whatever they were. It was an excuse to leave the Hillstead today. She knew it.

Denzel's cool look and easing back said he knew it too. "Alright then. I'll get Nan to watch the kids."

"Oh." The shock hit her brain again. Of course, he would have clients today. Saturday was when everyone was out of school, or in some cases, work. She'd blocked any consideration of his schedule from her brain. "D, I'm sorry, I just..."

"Forgot. I know." His smile was forgiving, infinitely so. Like it always was.

She didn't deserve it. Not after a year. Her face heated. "I'll make it up to you."

"You'll do no such thing." He leaned in and kissed her cheek, swiftly. "You go do what you gotta do today. I know you miss her. I know nothing's going to put that right. But whatever you feel you have to do about it, that's what you should do. We'll talk tonight."

The kids' song must have ended because suddenly, they were swarming up behind him, grabbing onto his legs, pulling on his arms. "I'm talking with your mom." His voice was as stern as it ever got —which was about as threatening as soft butter—and it didn't slow them down one bit.

"You gotta come!" Jayden insisted.

"I'm dancing," Audre reported in, twirling with her arms raised, round and round. That was headed for disaster.

"Alright, one more, then Daddy's gotta go to work. You're staying with Nan today."

"Yes!" Jayden threw his hands up then clasped them together, giving thanks in the way five-year-olds do for fervently offered prayers that have been answered. Nan's house was a rule-free zone—her mother spoiled the kids mercilessly. It was harder to get them to come home than it was getting them there. "Now?" Jayden demanded, all thoughts of dancing vaporized.

"Soon." Denzel waved them toward the stairs. "I know you'd rather Nan adopted you outright. Go get dressed, so you at least look like we take care of you."

Jayden took off running. Audre was still twirling. Denzel caught her just as she was teetering into the table, then swooped her up into his arms. Her head wobbled.

"Pocket sound, Audre, mute," he said, loudly, then in a normal voice. "We're going to Nan's, baby."

"Yay!" She lifted her still-chubby arms briefly, then grabbed onto Denzel's neck as the vertigo hit.

He laughed and held her with a hand splayed

across her back to keep her steady. The smile faded as he looked at Zuri. "You know Ruby's performance is coming up. A week from today."

Amani's daughter. Her niece. "I know."

His face fell even more serious. "You should be there, Zuri. She needs her Auntie."

She needs her mom. Instead, the woman who looked like her mom, but wasn't, would be in the audience. Sometimes Zuri was the ghost. "I'll be there." Even she could hear the hesitation that would turn into excuses later. "I have it on my calendar."

He frowned a little. "Are you sure you want to go in to work today?"

She pulled in a breath and tried to put on a face that said, *Everything's fine!* "I just have this one meeting, then the rest I can do at home. I won't be long."

Denzel nodded like he believed none of it, especially not the promise to show up for Ruby's performance, and he had a right to every inch of that skepticism. She'd avoided seeing the girl almost entirely since the funeral. Which was no small feat given they lived next door.

She was a terrible Auntie. Barely functional mother. Half-present wife. The list in her brain of the relationships she was failing at was extensive.

Half of her was gone, and no matter how much she looked in the mirror, the other half was never there.

She blinked as she watched Denzel carry Audre toward the stairs. She'd missed the moment when he'd turned away. She wanted to call out her good-byes, but it was too late. Instead, she hustled to the front door, slipped on her work pumps, checked her look in the mirror—plain black slacks, simple cream-colored silk blouse—and decided it was acceptable for a meeting with an intern. Her hair might be frizzed at the ends, but it didn't show. Finger-combing smoothed out where she'd pulled. She kept her jewelry box by the front door, shedding the skin of formality right there when she came home, so it was easy enough to dress it up with her pearl cluster earrings and the triple string pearl necklace. The base station for her chip was also stored at the door, so she slid that into her pocket and hurried out the door, escaping before Denzel came back downstairs with the kids.

That morning sun she saw through the window put a glare on the Hillstead, making the small houses gleam, the walkways between them sparkle, and even the clover lawn in the center had shine. Zuri shielded her eyes and watched her step—the hard-scrabble, natural surface of the pathways through the

Hillstead were ecologically sound but hell on heels. It fit the building code, so that's what mattered. The Firestead Act of 2040 bought up land in Southern California's fire-ravaged canyons, long after most people had moved on, and parceled it out to new owners who pledged to improve the ecology and fire safety of their land and the publicly-owned lands surrounding it. Lamar Hill, legendary showrunner in Hollywood and her father, knew a good deal when he saw it. He entered the lottery and snagged a five-acre parcel. He and Nan retired to the Hillstead, as he dubbed it, and built a half dozen small homes around the common area. Unlike most co-housing lots in the suburbs or even the eco-villages that had sprouted up around the country, Firesteads were unique with their strict regulations and high maintenance costs—as well as being almost entirely off the grid. They'd had to pay to bury a cable all the way down to the main grid junction, but nearly every surface of the Hillstead's structures was building-integrated photovoltaics: solar skins, solar fabric, and the more traditional panels plus a fleet of battery storage. Enough that they easily met their 90% statutory target for self-reliance.

Which was important not just to keep in the good graces of the State of Southern California. It would be embarrassing if the Greater Los Angeles Area Regional Director of the United States Energy Consortium was violating her energy contract. USEC would care a lot more about how *that* looked than a few stray kilowatts of over-usage.

"Where you going this beautiful morning?" Auntie Cora's voice jerked Zuri's attention up. She was out on her porch with her wife, Vivian, whose round body was wrapped in a brilliant purple smock as she painted. Vivian was a graphic designer before retiring, and now she worked with climate refugees on developing their art skills. The brilliant colorscape she was creating must be related to that.

Zuri squinted against the sun. "Just going in to work for a bit." She kept walking, eyes on her path, praying the Aunties wouldn't waylay her as they usually did.

"But it's Saturday," Cora objected.

"You're one to talk." Zuri gestured to the parts of a disassembled robotic arm splayed out on the tea table. Cora was retired, but she shared the same engineering gene as Zuri and her mother, and she was the Hillstead's self-appointed bot technician. Zuri had heard all the details before. This project was some kind of painting bot that demonstrated techniques to assist Vivian in teaching the refugees.

"*Cora,*" Vivian shushed, her attention pulled from the easel. Her brush hovered over the canvas, her sleek, straightened hair bound up in a top knot to keep it out of the way. "Zuri has important work to do. Don't go hassling her."

"Well, I know that." Cora's full silver afro was a contrast to her slim body and nimble fingers, now tapping the table to emphasize her point. "I was just asking."

"Some days, you shouldn't ask." Vivian focused on her easel again, swiping a streak of blue across the center, but she raised her voice for Zuri. "You go on, girl. Do what you gotta do."

It made Zuri wince—Cora was the kind who might forget today was the anniversary of Amani's death, but not Vivian.

Zuri was already hustling past their tidy porch and ignoring Cora's scowl. "I'll be back by the afternoon!" She waved without looking and just kept going, striding past her mother's house and Granddaddy Terrell's. He was her husband's grandfather—Zuri's father brought him onto the Hillstead so they could all keep an eye on him. But the man was already eighty-five and probably would outlive them all.

It wasn't right that Amani was gone before him.

That thought made no sense, but it still floated in Zuri's mind, like toxic oil seeping up from the depths. Amani and Zuri were A-to-Z, peace and beauty, as her father always reminded them. They were bookends, Amani vivacious where Zuri was reserved. Amani was an artist, Zuri an engineer—they fit the way her Aunties did, balancing each other. And now... it was like the world's spin was off, wobbling from the missing mass of her sister's presence.

Zuri was trapped in that thought vortex until she reached the Hillstead's entrance... and the car was gone. *"Shit."* She just stared blankly at the empty spot for a moment.

"Mrs. Hill took it," a soft voice said behind her.

Zuri whipped around and nearly stumbled when a rock twisted her heel. She righted herself then peered at the tiny guest house at the edge of the Hillstead. The kid—Michael, one of Denzel's clients—lurked in the doorway, gangly and tall, his face shadowed by the solar fabric awning above, but the sun lit up the lower half of him, from his pale, bare arms to his rumpled gray sweats. He was only seventeen but already had one parent suicide out, the other on drugs, and his grandma had a heart attack, which was how he ended up with them. Just a white kid trying to make it in a tough LA neighborhood with no chance. The Hillstead was a safe harbor until he got his feet under him. Remote school. A place to live. Denzel was encouraging him to apply for college in the fall, but it was hard for the kid to see a future when his past was nothing but a wasteland.

"Hey," Zuri said, trying to soften her voice. "You're saying Nan Hill took the car?"

A small motion in the shadow looked like a nod. "About an hour ago."

"Okay. Thanks."

The boy slipped back inside.

Zuri cursed, silently this time, then swiped the air to bring up a virtual keyboard. *Nan took the car,* she messaged to Denzel. *Kids will have to stay with the Aunties.* She swiped it away and sighed. Now she was complicating *everyone's* day. But they weren't the only Firestead in Topanga, and the canyon kept a small fleet of autocars for community use. Luckily, one was available. She hailed it and set off down the Hillstead's driveway to the main road. It was a good quarter-mile, and her heels were *not* made for this, but at first, the steady drumbeat of them on the compacted dirt helped drive off the guilt. Then the heat of the sun and the view of the distant California shores, sparkling and beautiful, cracked open a door for the recriminations to push their way in.

She lived on the top of a damn mountain with a million-dollar view, she'd already succeeded beyond her wildest dreams in her career, and she had a big, loving, crazy-amazing family. Her life was everyone's dream, and her home was a refuge that kids like Michael came to in order to recover from the *true* hardships they'd endured. And it worked—Zuri was sure Denzel would see him through, just as he had the dozen before him. Her husband was a grief counselor, for heaven's sake, and exceptionally good at his job. Why couldn't his magic—and the magic of the Hillstead—work for her?

Why was she still, a year on, hollow inside?

The autocar arrived just as she thought she might have to abandon her shoes by the side of the road. The ride down the canyon was short and winding, dulling out her negative self-talk with the swaying and the heat. Weekend traffic was snarled on the new PCH—the original Pacific Coast Highway having been washed away a decade ago— but once she hit Santa Monica and turned inland on the 10, traffic was lighter. Rail and bike were how most people moved through the city. Only rich "important" jerks like her used cars and clogged the highways with a single passenger on board. But getting to USEC would have been a two-hour jaunt otherwise. It was a perk she gladly used.

Still, she would be late, so she messaged Jeevika to make excuses for her... then she got her brain out of the fog of recriminations and into work mode. She brought up the file on the intern she was meeting: *Yoram Brin.* He was a power engineering student, born in NYC before the flooding, attended the Institute in LA where Zuri graduated what felt like ages ago. Her class of 2037 was among the first to matriculate from the newly-founded Institute, and most of her classrooms were in buildings partially under construction. She'd briefly interviewed young Yoram for an internship for the summer at Power Island Four. He seemed intelligent and responsible. Honestly, she hardly remembered him. But he apparently was having some kind of personnel crisis that required her intervention. That happened more often than one might think in an organization dedicated to machinery and power generation.

By the time the autocar exited the freeway toward downtown LA and the IEC complex—the International Energy Consortium housed USEC, the World Science Organization, the UN's various climate panels, and more—her head was fully engaged in speculation about what flavor of problem Yoram was bringing to her. Sexual harassment? Anti-Semitism? Bigotry of some other kind? As much as humanity had made progress since she was born in 2015—a tumultuous, often violent process, especially with the pressures of the climate crisis and the endless wave of pandemics—there were still holdouts who believed their skin color or sexual orientation or religion made them superior. That shit was unacceptable and had to stay out of the workplace—especially *her* workplace. She wouldn't put up with it, but even more important, USEC's work was too critical to let biases corrupt it. If Yoram's "personnel" problem was of that kind, it would be easy enough to deal with. But she suspected something less dramatic. Probably some office romance gone wrong, although when she checked his file, his start date wasn't until next week. *Strange.*

USEC was housed in the iconic central IEC building, which gleamed as she approached. The massive structure was reminiscent of a wave, the architect having in mind both the ocean waves surrounding Energy Island when it was first formed and the symbolic waves of the pandemics that drove the IEC's creation. It was huge, but an entire wing was devoted to USEC. Zuri punched in navigation to the basement parking lot. There weren't many spaces, but she'd rather have it recharge and wait for her than have to call it back.

Her office was on the 3rd floor of the low building. On the way up, she let Jeevika know she'd arrived. Her assistant messaged back that she'd cleared Yoram through to wait in the office. Security was tighter on the weekend with the tourist crowds coming through, so Zuri had to pass a full voice-print-facial-scan three times on the way in. But when she waved open the door to her office, she stopped short.

Yoram wasn't alone.

He had a young woman—mid-twenties—with him who was vaguely familiar. They both were gawking at her view of the city and the shores beyond and turned quickly when she entered.

"Yoram?" she asked in a tone that said he had about two seconds to explain, or she was calling security. *How did this person even get past the identity checks?*

"Madam Director," Yoram rushed out, scuttling across the carpet of her office. "This is Lucía Ramirez, power engineer at Power Island One."

Zuri's alarm stepped back from the cliff. "I see." She flicked a finger to activate a search, but even before Ms. Ramirez's file popped up, Zuri remembered where she'd seen her before. A transfer down from Oregon, Power Island 43, not long ago. Sexual harassment case. Zuri had an opening on Power Island One, approved the transfer, and that was it. How was Yoram involved in this?

Ramirez stepped forward, bowing formally, arms at her side, gaze dropped. But when she looked up, she said rather breathlessly, "Madam Director. We need your help. Someone at Power Island One is stealing power from the grid."

"*Stealing.*" Zuri didn't know what was going on here, but—

"And they tried to kill me."

Zuri just blinked.

TWO

Zuri listened with half her attention.

The other half of her mind was spinning alternate theories—*sane* theories—which could explain why a power engineer was standing in her office spouting wild accusations she sincerely hoped were not based in fact. Because if any of this was true, Zuri's life would get immeasurably more complicated.

The last thing she needed right now was complications.

"I've got pictures of everything," Lucía Ramirez continued, her voice way too steady and calm for the words she was saying. "The replacement parts for the repairs they said never happened. The secret cable siphoning power from the mainland grid." She narrowed her eyes at Zuri. "This is just a copy." She handed over a slim storage drive.

Zuri took it with an arched eyebrow. "You don't trust me."

Yoram, the young intern, was already twitchy as a kitten. His eyes popped open at Zuri's tone.

"Someone tried to kill me yesterday," Lucía said, locking gazes with Zuri. "I sincerely hope it wasn't you."

Zuri scowled. But if nothing else, it was clear *Lucía* believed she'd been attacked. "All right," she sighed, "Let's back this up." The glare coming off the nearby buildings was grating on her nerves. *"Windows, 50%,"* she instructed, then gestured for Lucía and Yoram to take a seat in the two upholstered chairs between her desk and the rounded windowscape. With the glare gone, Zuri could settle into her chair, lace her fingers, and study the two for a moment. Yoram was still in college, slight, pale skin drained even more white. He was still spooked like he thought the seats might be rigged for electric shocks. Lucía wasn't much older, mid-twenties, but she had a calm confidence Zuri recognized. *Girl knew her stuff.* Zuri flicked a finger through the air, paging through Lucía's file, which had been waiting in her peripheral vision, just to refresh her memory.

Ah, yes. Zuri had approved the transfer to Power Island One, a plum position, in part because Lucía was legacy. Her parents had both worked—and died—on the Island. Lucía had grown up there until the plague took her family. *Arctic Thaw Paleovirus-34.* The world saw the danger of viruses releasing from the thawing permafrost for decades yet somehow was unprepared when it finally hit... including the Hill twins. Zuri got sick, but Amani nearly died. Months in the hospital, Amani in an induced coma, Zuri by her side. Zuri thought maybe they would just die there, like that, together. In the end, they survived when many others did not. But did they, really? Sixteen years later, Amani dropped dead in her kitchen while eating oatmeal with blueberries, her daughter Ruby screaming until Marcel came running. Massive blot clot in the brain, one of the common after-effects of ATP-34. Zuri knew before the autopsy, before she even heard what happened. *She felt it.*

That and she heard the screaming next door.

Zuri had never believed in those "mystical twin bonds" people spoke about, but that morning, no one had to tell her Amani had died. Or how.

Amani stared from the dimmed window, her fingers laced, expression blank. *Why do you think I wanted to be in that longitudinal study of survivors?* Amani needled her.

Zuri was still part of the study. Amani was one of their statistics.

Didn't help you. Zuri almost said the words aloud, then caught herself.

Lucía and Yoram were staring at her.

Zuri cleared her throat. "So, let's see if I have this right. You think someone has laid a secret power cable between Power Island One and the mainland, and they're siphoning off power to run secret fusion experiments in secret underground labs on the Island."

Lucía frowned. "Well, we can't be sure it was fusion. They burned down the labs."

"Burned them down. And no one noticed this?" Zuri knew those labs, even if she hadn't been there in a decade. There were plenty of fire prevention and suppression systems.

Yoram piped up. "They gave Lucía a one-day suspension, off-Island, during the fire. You know... to cover it up..." He faltered, dashing a look to Lucía, who just shook her head.

"So, we have disciplinary actions involved." Zuri was trying to give them a fair hearing, but this was too crazy. And she didn't have emotional room for anyone else's crazy right now.

Lucía's frown turned hard. "It was an excuse to get me off the Island."

"So they could cover things up." Zuri tapped the air to bring up the disciplinary section of Lucía's file, and sure enough, there was a whole page detailing the event.

"You're a power engineer." Lucía's change in tone jerked Zuri's attention away from the file.

"I was." Zuri squinted. What did she mean by that?

"On Power Island One," Lucía continued. "In the early days, when it was still Energy Island. You graduated from the Institute, did pioneering work on fusion on the Island, quickly rose through the ranks, and now you're here."

"Is there a point to this, Ms. Ramirez?" A short trip of alarm went through Zuri's mind. There were no skeletons in her closet, nothing for a young power engineer to hold over her, but if there was anything to this wild tale Lucía was telling... it was happening on her watch. And the last year had been, well, *a haze*. If someone was hatching schemes under her nose, it would be more than embarrassing—it would mean she wasn't doing her job. Maybe not even capable of it anymore. *Broken*. And that thought had to be hacked up and buried immediately because she was *not* entertaining it.

"In all your time as a power engineer," Lucía continued, not seeming to notice how Zuri had straightened a little in her chair, "have you ever had a portion of the Island off-limits?"

"Well, private quarters—"

"I'm talking laboratories. Storage areas. Any part of the Island used for official business. Because once you have clearance to the Island, you're there to keep things running. There are no secret, off-limits areas in the basement. Not for adults. Not for *power engineers.*"

True enough. "And you're saying there were. On Power Island One."

"A whole rabbit warren of them, behind the James B. Ellis Fusion Museum, guarded by a surly volunteer historian named Johannes Casimir. And I got a one-day suspension simply for poking around, trying to find out exactly what was in those supposed storage areas. Does that sound right to you?"

"No," Zuri admitted. "It does not." She turned her attention back to the write-up on Lucía's suspension. *"Insubordination. Not adjusting well. Accusa-*

tions against other power engineers on the Island. Violating clearance."

"Now, why would I need clearance to look in a storage area?"

Zuri swiped the file closed. "It sounds like there was more going on than just that."

"There was." But Lucía obviously meant it differently than she did.

"Ms. Ramirez, I'm sorry, but this is all just a bit... *fantastical.*" One thing Lucía had said jumped out to Zuri as the first of many potential holes in her story. "First of all, there's no volunteer historian on Power Island One. I would have approved something like that, and I haven't."

"I know," she said. "I checked the records. He's not officially listed anywhere."

"That's convenient."

Lucía sighed, obviously frustrated, and gripped the seat of her chair as she leaned slightly forward. "Yesterday, *someone* vented 90% of the air out of my tank, tampered with the indicator, and drained my emergency tank to zero. The only reason I'm here at all is..." She stalled out, anger eating her words as she stared at a point somewhere in the middle of Zuri's desk.

Yoram put a hand on her shoulder, his concern obvious.

"I'm okay," Lucía said softly.

Zuri felt the sting of guilt, but that was a constant friend. And she needed to say the obvious. "Are you sure it wasn't just... an accident?"

Lucía dragged her gaze up to meet hers. "Do you dive, Madam Director?"

"No."

"There is zero chance I would drain my own emergency tank."

"That does seem unlikely."

Lucía shook her head, exchanged a wordless, brief conversation with Yoram that seemed to debate whether they should simply get up and leave Zuri's office. The sting of guilt spread its poison, clamping down on her chest. Before she could say anything, Lucía looked at her again.

"We had to take the chance that you might be involved." She gestured to the drive still in Zuri's hand. "Astra Olson, lead engineer on the VIV—the Vortex Induced Vibrations machinery that was secretly repaired—she's in the pictures. She, well, she helped drag me out of the water, but she's involved. She said as much. Miller Zendek is definitely covering for Casimir. I don't why, Madam Director. I don't know what was hidden down in those old fusion labs, I don't know what sliced up the VIV or why they're so determined to cover it up, and I don't know how they could have laid an undersea cable without someone in USEC knowing what they're up to—and covering for them. But I know that unscheduled, rolling blackouts across the Los Angeles Metro Area are something no Regional Director would want happening on their watch."

"Is that a threat, Ms. Ramirez?"

Lucía blinked. Innocent. Like Zuri had just accused her of something which had never occurred to her. "No, ma'am."

And at that moment... *Zuri believed her.* It might all be delusion, or maybe a whole wild set of coincidences with some logical explanation, but Lucía believed it all. And having a power engineer who believed in some grand conspiracy afoot on her Power Island was a complication Zuri couldn't simply dismiss.

Plus, there was one other thing. "You said Miller Zendek is involved in this?"

"He has to be," Lucía insisted, her hands now balled up on her knees, holding her tension with a death grip. "When I brought him the report on the VIV—how it had been damaged—he totally dismissed it. And then, *twenty-four hours later,* it was fixed. Same with the blackouts on the mainland. Once I'd reported it *to him,* they stopped. Not to mention that *disciplinary report,*" she ground out through her teeth.

"All right." Zuri held up her hand to stop her before she got any more wound up. If there was anything not-quite-savory happening at Power Island One, Zuri had no problem believing Miller was part of it. They had a history, as her mother would say. That, and he was the Island's designer, ostensibly in charge of the entire operation. Zuri had a dozen Power Islands under her purview. She relied on the designers to manage their Islands but also to give her accurate information about their problems as they arose.

Miller never brought her anything. That alone would be suspicious if she didn't know he liked to play power games and felt himself just a little above reporting to the Regional Director.

Especially when it was her.

"Go home," Zuri told the two of them. "Sit tight while I—"

"I can't," Lucía said.

"Sorry?"

"Miller has the coordinates of the cottage where

I live." She exchanged a look with Yoram, who looked ready to protest, then turned back to Zuri with resolve on her face. "Someone's trying to kill me. I need to relocate in case he comes after me again."

Zuri pressed her lips together. This was a complication she didn't need. But she also didn't need one of her power engineers making the news for fleeing her home. *Or* ending up dead, if this all wasn't delusion or mistake. "All right, look. You can stay at my family's Firestead. I'll send you the coordinates. My mother has an extra room. You'll be fine there while I sort this out."

Lucía's expression had opened in surprise. "You would do that?"

"Don't thank me until you've had some of my mother's cooking." But she rose up from her seat, indicating that it was time for them to go.

Lucía and Yoram hustled to their feet.

"Thank you, Madam Director," Yoram gushed. The boy looked even more relieved than Lucía.

"That's really generous of you." Lucía still seemed shocked. "I appreciate it." Then her frown returned. "What are you going to do?"

Zuri waved them toward the door. "Sounds like I

need to make an unscheduled visit to the designer of Power Island One."

Lucía and Yoram exchanged another look, this time tinged with hope. Then they made their bows and scurried out of her office.

Zuri closed the door behind them, turned to lean against it, then sighed at the drive in her hand, the one with Lucía's pictures. "I did *not* need this mess today," she muttered to her empty office then let out a long, low breath.

You solve seven catastrophes before breakfast! Amani's voice reached through her memories from a sunny afternoon on the Hillstead, a rare one she had taken off.

"That was the old me. New me is *tired*." She was arguing with a ghost.

Not a good sign.

Zuri rubbed her face and braced herself for the trip to Power Island One. Miller would *not* enjoy her poking into his business.

That was the only good thing about this.

THREE

THE BRIGHT SUN AND WARM SEA BREEZE WERE A nature-driven hard reboot to her brain.

Zuri's shoulders relaxed. She breathed in the salty air. Even the sway of the Coastal Patrol boat was soothing. The splash of waves and the cry of gulls reminded her just how much she missed living on the Islands.

Even though she worked on the mainland now, Zuri tried to visit the Power Islands under her purview at least once a year.

How long had it been?

She honestly couldn't remember without consulting her calendar.

Too long. Obviously.

That nudged up thoughts about how much

mischief someone like Miller Zendek could get up to unsupervised. And how this grief that had seized hold of her might actually be compromising her work. Which was so unacceptable, she didn't know what to do with it.

Zuri closed her eyes as the boat neared the dock on Power Island One. She tipped her head up, soaked in the sun on her face, and pulled the fresh air into her lungs. Whatever had happened over the last year, she was here now, today... and she would get to the bottom of whatever this mess was about, clean it up, and get back home before dinner.

The Coastal Patrol boat eased up to the dock, and Zuri opened her eyes just as a crewmember hurried past. The Patrol was separate from the US Coast Guard and under the exclusive jurisdiction of the IEC—the International Energy Consortium—a compromise made when the first Energy Island was established in 2028. Back then, the Island was anchored in international waters, a massive scientific endeavor to accelerate clean energy tech, including fusion.

Zuri had only been thirteen, but she remembered the excitement—and the horror that drove it. The world was being crushed by pandemics, and that spurred an incredible international agreement, ambitious in scope like nothing since the European Recovery Program after World War II. Only this was an attempt to save the entire world from climate-driven plagues. The World Health Organization spawned off the WSO—the World Science Organization—specifically to deal with the medical side of the pandemic threats. Early identification, rapid vaccine development, massive investment in the technology to fight this biological warfare that wasn't country vs. country but humanity vs. a microscopic enemy... and the consequences of their addiction to carbon-emitting fuels.

At the same time, the IEC formed to guide investment in Energy Island and to broker agreements for sharing the dividends of the research. Every nation contributed funds, and every one had input into the decision-making. Unlike the United Nations' other climate panels, this one didn't measure the impact of or warn about the coming catastrophes—it was hands-on solving the problem. That meant generating clean energy of every kind, as well as scalable technology to extract carbon from the air and sequester it again.

The IEC's shiny new building in Los Angeles housed representatives from around the world, focusing all the various international climate efforts.

Energy Island sizzled with innovation, but fusion never reached its potential—more important, the battery technology breakthrough meant industrial energy storage had finally arrived. Zuri had only been on the Island three years, assisting her mother in fusion research, when the labs were shut down, and Energy Island became Power Island One. It was towed into US waters, and USEC was mandated to put all the green tech wonders into production, scaling up quickly to dozens of Islands, up and down the coasts. Other countries did the same.

Today, as she stepped off the Patrol boat in her ill-suited work heels, the crewmember standing ready to give her a hand, Power Island One was simply one of hundreds of Power Islands around the world, all producing the clean energy necessary to drag humanity back from the precipice of climate disaster. Not that they'd made it yet. The US had been stalled out at 80% renewables for five years. That last 20% was vexing. A few anti-conservation zealots trafficked in shale oil from the north or kept illicit propane tanks for their off-grid ranches, but mostly, it was jet fuel and the plastics industry. Electric planes were still limited to smaller craft, and some petroleum-based products were still extremely difficult to replace. Plus, clean energy from the

Power Islands and all the onshore renewables—solar grids, wind farms, hydroelectric—could barely keep up with the world's energy needs. There wasn't enough capacity, even now in 2050, after decades of building out infrastructure, to carbon-capture the emissions from all the dirty energy sources still left.

Every bit of clean power counted. Every kilowatt was *necessary*. If someone was indeed siphoning power from the grid, Zuri would put a stop to it.

She just couldn't imagine who would do such a thing or why. Even Miller Zendek.

It made no sense.

As she marched past the orchard and its weeding bots, she logged into the Island's system and pulled up the locator. Miller was in the old James B. Ellis building where Zuri and her mother had worked alongside dozens of other scientists and engineers, supporting the fusion operation. Physicists like Ellis floated in from time to time, checking results and equipment, but it was engineers like her and scientists like her mother who ran the day-to-day operations of the miniature star they ignited but could never quite sustain. Years of her life were down in those *rabbit warrens* as Lucía described them. Zuri wasn't sentimental about that, but a fire damaging the old labs was unsettling... and easy enough to fact-check before she surprised Miller with her presence. The locator said he was on the second floor, so when she reached the boxy glass building, she quietly stole to the elevator and took it down to the basement.

The smell hit her first. Stale air and carbon.

Then the sight of the scorch marks around the partially-open museum door. It was nothing but darkness beyond, the light from the elevator not piercing it, but Zuri didn't need to see any more.

She slowly eased back into the elevator and pushed the button to return to the main floor.

What was the timeline on this?

Zuri pulled up Lucía's file for the 10th time. The girl claimed her suspension was an excuse to get her off-Island for the fire. Which meant it happened during that time. When the elevator dinged and opened, Zuri was still scanning the record for a time-stamp. *Wednesday,* but in the evening. Suspension was Thursday, when the fire supposedly occurred. Today was Saturday, mid-afternoon. Zuri had more than a passing familiarity with what fire could do—living on a Firestead came with lots of training, including being your own volunteer on-location fire department. She was no expert in forensics, but according to Lucía's timeline, this fire was approximately 48 hours old. That tracked with how it *smelled,* although the controlled burns in the canyon left a lingering scent for a lot longer than two days. Had it happened long ago, the Island's maintenance bots would have been down here, cleaning it up. She should have had a report on her desk within an hour of when it was contained.

With renewed purpose, she strode toward the stairs and the coordinates of one Miller Zendek. The Island's locator placed him in an office upstairs. The door was closed, but she could hear the shouting even before she got close. Given she hadn't seen a soul since leaving the boat, meaning no one was likely to see her spying, she quieted her steps and eased up to listen.

"You need me down there!" It was a woman's voice.

"I'm already missing one engineer." Miller's tone was his usual clipping arrogance, although angrier than she'd heard in a while. "Which is a *hell* of a problem, Astra."

"What was I supposed to do?" It was a whine.

"You *know* what you were supposed to do." Miller was *pissed.*

"How was I... I couldn't just..." She trailed off.

Miller's groan sounded frustrated. "You know what? *Fine.* We'll deal with it. I'm *not* letting this screw everything. We're too close. We just need to pull together another few runs with better controls—"

"Which is why I need to be there!" There was desperation to that plea.

"No! *You* need to stay here and unfuck this situation. Ellis can get by just fine without you."

"That wasn't our agreement!" Her whining was getting angrier.

"Our agreement..." There was a pause, and Zuri had to strain to hear Miller's lowered tone. "...is what I say it is. Don't make me decide you're expendable in this project. Are we clear?"

Zuri held her breath, waiting for more, but if Astra said anything, she couldn't hear it. Suddenly, footsteps were scuffing their way to the door. Zuri hastily knocked, not wanting to be caught eavesdropping.

The footsteps stopped. There was a long pause.

Then the door yanked inward. Miller's angry expression looked ready to curse her out until he realized who was standing outside the door. His eyes flew wide, and a brief but very satisfying look of utter panic flashed across his face. Then he locked everything down, his smile tighter than the tolerances on a fusion reactor and holding back just as much energy.

"Zuri!" he exclaimed with an impressive amount of exuberance and also the usual over-familiarity he always used with her. As if she were still an intern on Energy Island. "To what do we owe the very special pleasure of your visit?" He flashed a look back to Astra, whose expression was somewhere between stark terror and actual death.

"Thought I'd check in on my favorite Power Island," Zuri said coolly. "Do you have a moment?" She stepped back, inviting him to leave the office, which was really a lab. Behind him, Zuri could see an impressive amount of hardware and a rack of servers easily a quarter the size of the Island's main computing system. She had no idea what Astra would need that for, given her main responsibilities were maintaining the VIV, which was run by repair bots down in the robotics hangar. Zuri had checked Astra's file, given she was in Lucía's cache of images —there was no need for substantial computing resources in her job description.

"Absolutely!" Miller enthused, quickly stepping outside the lab and closing the door, unceremoniously cutting off Astra's shocked expression. "It's been too long, Zuri. How are your family up on the Hillstead? I heard about the loss of your sister. I hope you got my heartfelt condolences. Such a terrible thing. And in front of her daughter, no less. I sincerely hope the grief has rested easily on you and your family."

"Same old Miller, I see." Although she expected the emotional manipulation—the pure *assault* Miller was so expert at—her stomach still churned with the punches.

"*Zuri.*" He frowned like he expected better from her. "I'm sure I have no idea what you mean."

"I'm sure you don't." She held his gaze and watched the calculation flick behind his eyes. They were the same age, and in the early days of Energy Island, they'd both been rising stars, but he'd never treated her as an equal. Even after she was promoted above him, he never even cynically switched gears to the fawning treatment she saw him dole out to those in positions of power. She could never tell if Miller's low opinion of her was because she was a woman or because she was a *Black* woman. It was never obvious enough or egregious enough to get him written up. He knew where the line was drawn, down to the millimeter, and he skated right up to it every time. She had learned early on not to give Miller Zendek any benefit of any doubt. The man enjoyed making a fool of you at checkers, all while he believed he was playing

14th-dimensional chess. Rules were for other people, and you were lucky if you knew what game was actually being played. Whatever he had going on with Astra, whether it had anything to do with Lucía or not, he was hiding *something*. He always was.

She waited long enough, let him squirm until it was painful enough he finally flinched. "All right. What have I done? Missed my monthly report?"

Zuri let herself smile a little, just because it might unnerve him. "I think you're missing Lucía Ramirez."

His plastered-on smile twitched. "I'm sure she's just gone home for the weekend."

"Actually, she's at the Hillstead right now."

He blinked. *Choked*, really. "Whatever she's told you—"

"Now, what would she tell me?"

The panicked look flashed back. She was enjoying this far too much. "Zuri—*Madam Director* —I was hoping to spare you this. But Ms. Ramirez is a troubled woman. We were trying to handle it on-Island—"

"Were you?"

"I *was*." It felt like the first sincere thing he'd said to her. "I know you're busy at USEC, especially given your personal circumstances. I was trying to spare you, Zuri. I swear. I'm not *hiding* anything."

She didn't believe that for a moment, but it was just plausible enough she had to entertain it. "Then get me up to speed."

Miller scowled. "I don't know what she's told you—"

"Just walk me through your version of things," she said coolly. "And we'll go from there."

She could feel the tension rolling off him, but he played it off with a shrug. "Where to begin?" He stepped over to the railing and peered at the towering racks of vegetables that fed the Island. In the early days, the entire glass building had been a bustling fusion research lab. Now, attendant bots marched dutifully down the rows of cabbage, stamping out weeds. "I'm sure you know she had, well, *trouble* up North."

"She was sexually harassed." If he even *tried* to make that Lucía's fault, Zuri would toss him over the edge. Figuratively. Probably.

"Of course. It's not her fault that she's a beautiful young woman who would attract that kind of predator." To the edge, but never crossing it. "But perhaps it left her... *unsettled.* From the moment she arrived, she was finding conspiracies everywhere. Even *before* she came to the Island." He waved his hand dismissively as he leaned back against the railing. "Something about random power outages that were destroying home-based battery backups." He squinted in disapproval. "That's the kind of thing you find on the chatter boards, not something I expect my power engineers to bring me."

"I'm assuming you investigated it, regardless." Lucía's drive of photos included the battery backups at her cottage that had been supposedly destroyed, but Zuri hadn't had time to investigate any of that. She'd come straight here.

"Sure. But you know as well as I that nothing like that could happen. Maybe once. Glitches happen. But the mainland grid AI would adaptively manage it right out of existence. I don't have to tell you that." He tipped his head to her. "Mainland grid management is the province of the Regional Director, after all."

Oh, hell no, he was not putting this on her. "So, based on that, you think Ms. Ramirez is... what did you call it? *Unsettled."*

He frowned, apparently displeased she didn't take his bait. "It was far more than that. She fabricated a report of damage to the VIV, and when we refused to fix something that wasn't broken, she went crawling all over the Island, looking for evidence of some grand conspiracy or coverup or something. I wrote it up—you should look at the report if you haven't already—and then I sent her off-Island to let her pull herself together." He straightened up from his casual lean, and his face drew down. "Zuri, I think she has some deep-seated need to get vengeance on the Island. As if she blames it—*us*—for what happened to her family. You know they died from ATP-34, right? Right here on the Island. *They never left.* It's like the ghosts of her family are *here,* Zuri."

That made her flinch.

Miller didn't seem to notice, bent on drilling home how off-balance Lucía was. "She must have left some kind of bomb or incendiary device here on the Island. I think she was planting it when my alert systems were triggered in the old fusion labs—they were closed off, too much hazardous material down there. I don't know what she was doing or why, but I never in a million years would have thought any power engineer, even one in the middle of a mental breakdown, would plant bombs on an Island. It was just inconceivable. I sent her off-Island without any idea how far gone she was. But it was only a few hours later that *something* exploded down there. We don't know what, but some kind of accelerant must have been used in the blast. Everything was engulfed, all at once, burning everything to ash. We barely kept it contained to the underground. You should go look."

"I've already been down there." *Lucía* set the fire? That seemed... crazy. Especially with her landing in Zuri's office, saying someone had tried to murder her. Which, honestly, was the hardest part to believe in this.

"You've seen it already?" Miller's eyebrows hiked up, and he seemed genuinely surprised. "Then you know. Everything's just gone. The museum, all the vintage stuff we had saved from the early days—*your* years in the fusion lab, Zuri—all gone."

Miller's attempt to make this personal, connecting to her past, pinged Zuri's suspicions again. *Same old Miller.* The manipulation came out whenever he was up to something. Which was *always.* "Why didn't you inform me?"

Miller threw out his hands in exasperation. "I was trying to work this out. Get the girl some help. What was I going to do, send the police to arrest her on the mainland? Splash that headline all across the news? You would have had my head."

She scowled. "Still doesn't explain why you didn't bring this to me right away."

He briefly rubbed his hand across his forehead. "All right. You're right. I should have done that. *I'm sorry*. I thought I could wait until she returned to the Island, confront her then, give her the option to go into voluntary hospitalization. Or involuntary, if she seemed like a danger to herself. Or the Island. I couldn't have her staying here for any length of time, obviously. I just... I thought I could handle it. Then she left the Island before I could meet with her, so I figured..." He shrugged. "Maybe she'd gone on the run. Or was getting some help. I had no idea she would come to *you*, Zuri, believe me—I would definitely have contacted you first."

She believed that if only to cover his tracks. "Well, she's in my custody now." She'd already messaged her mother, who confirmed that Lucía had arrived at the Hillstead.

"I'd be careful," Miller said with the sincerity of a snake. "She's not stable. Who knows what story she'll make up to explain all this. I wouldn't want anything to happen to your family. You've been through enough. Maybe we should go ahead and trigger a mental health evaluation. Start the documentation at least."

Miller was rambling now, searching for anything to contain the situation with Lucía—whatever the exact nature of that was. That alone made Zuri believe her more than him. But attempted murder? Over what? She still had no clue.

Which meant she needed a hell of a lot more information... and she would not get it from Miller Zendek. "She'll be fine at the Hillstead for now. I'll take it from here, Miller."

That made him plaster on an uncomfortable smile. "If you're sure—"

"I'm sure." She gestured back to the closed door to the lab. "And I'd like a word with your power engineer, as well. In private."

His eyes widened slightly. "Astra's not involved in any of this. I mean, sure, the VIV is her domain, but she—"

"Are you saying you don't want me to talk to her?" She arched an eyebrow.

"No, not at all." He swept a hand toward the door, but his jaw was clenched. "Go ahead. And if there's anything I can do to help with Lucía, just let me know. She is *my* power engineer, after all. I'm concerned for her."

Sure, you are. "I'll keep you informed of my investigation."

Miller seemed to struggle for words, which was a thing to see on him. "Great," he finally managed, then turned and headed for the stairs.

Zuri stepped up to the door but waited a moment, taking a deep breath to clear the Miller-stress out of her system. The man was a piece of work under normal circumstances. Whatever this was had all his worst features dialed up to maximum voltage. But that didn't mean he was out to murder his power engineer. Could she have read this all wrong? Was Lucía trapped in some mental break-down vortex that had caused her to come unraveled right as she returned to the Island where her family died? It wasn't inconceivable.

Zuri was all too familiar with the power of ghosts.

Except that didn't line up. Lucía came off angry and competent—not unhinged. And she had a picture of Astra on the docks, looking furious as Lucía left the Island just the night before. The images were time and geo-stamped. If nothing else, Zuri had solid evidence Astra was the last to see Lucía leave the Island.

Zuri waited as Miller's footsteps receded. The distant ding of the elevator said he was going to the burnt-out fusion labs. Interesting. She knocked lightly on the laboratory door.

After a moment, Astra pulled open the door and seemed surprised to see her.

"Ms. Olson, do you have a minute?"

Astra peered nervously around her, validating Zuri's hunch she needed to talk to Astra alone. "Sure. Okay." She stepped back, but Zuri didn't need to come inside.

She just had one pointed question she needed answered. "Does Miller know about the photos?"

"I'm sorry, what?" Her hand was nervously working the pocket of the white labcoat that hung on her thin frame.

"Lucía said someone tried to kill her yesterday." Zuri watched Astra's eyes slowly widen. "But she said *you* saved her. Pulled her from the water and put her on a boat to the mainland. The last picture she took was of you standing on the dock." Zuri leaned a little closer. Astra seemed to be holding her breath. "So, I'll ask you again. Does Miller know about the photos?"

She swallowed, hesitated, then shook her head in a tiny, mouse-like motion.

Zuri softened her voice. "You don't have to cover for him, Astra. I can protect you."

"I'm not—" Her voice cracked. She cleared her throat and spoke more forcefully. "I'm not covering for anyone."

It was such an obvious lie. "Think about it. You know where to find me."

Astra didn't respond, just stared like she'd been frozen in place, a tiny mouse in a very large box. Whatever this was, Astra was in deep. And Zuri was even more convinced Miller was hiding something major—maybe something worth killing for, although she couldn't imagine what. Death was permanent, *real* in a way none of Miller's games ever could be. It rippled out and touched people far and wide, leaving desolation in its wake. With pandemics ripping through the world, death was everywhere, ever-present. No one was untouched. To her, nothing could ever be worth adding to that horrible toll. Then again, some people thought power and money were worth dying for, so what did she know?

Not enough, apparently. But she would soon.

Zuri turned and left Astra hanging in the doorway.

FOUR

The sun was flirting with the horizon as Zuri's autocar pulled up to the Hillstead.

A trip into the city, then to Power Island One, then back again, would have been enough to wear her out—especially given how much of the last year she'd worked from home—but the day was far from done. Before she climbed out of the car, she pulled up a virtual keyboard to message her assistant, Jeevika.

Not going to review any reports today, she typed. *That personnel problem got real messy, real fast. I've got a power engineer staying with me at the Hillstead. Fill you in later.*

Everything can wait until Monday! Jeevika's response came right back. *"You wanna fly, you gotta give up the shit that's weighing you down." – Toni Morrison*

Zuri shook her head. *No more inspirational quotes unless I ask for them.* She regretted it as soon as she sent it.

Tough day if you're booting Toni. Message received, Boss!

Sorry, I'm having a moment... she typed, then erased it. She couldn't explain this day, and Jeevika didn't need to deal with it, anyway.

Instead, she sent a quick message to her husband. *Back at the Hillstead. Need to stop at Nan's first. Crazy day.*

Kids and I are making pizza, Denzel messaged back. *I'll fight them off to save you a piece.*

Zuri smiled and pulled in a deep breath. If Miller was actually right, and Lucía was having some kind of breakdown, she could pass this over to Denzel. He would make sure the girl was taken care of. But even as she thought that, she dismissed it. Miller was hiding something, Astra was in deep, and Lucía was the canary in the coal mine. Zuri just had to figure out what was about to blow up.

She climbed out of the car and sent it back to the canyon's fleet storage, then waved at Michael, her husband's patient, but the kid disappeared back inside his tiny cottage. She trudged down the path, longing for the moment she could ditch her shoes. Her mother's house was small, two steps up to the porch, and a bright red front door. They had a no-knock policy if you were expected, so Zuri cruised right in, only to find her mother and Lucía standing side-by-side, furiously grabbing at the air, laughing and shouting for no reason she could see.

"Oh, are you *kidding* me?"

"Don't you even—"

"What? There is *no* reason for that line to go down!"

"*Line?* Girl, I've got a whole sector that just got blown." That was her mother.

It took a moment for Zuri to figure it out. "Are you seriously making Lucía play SubGrid?"

Lucía turned toward her voice, but she was wearing blackout goggles. They were in virtual together. "Oh, uh, sorry, Madam Director—"

"*Madam Director* can wait—you need to build that substation!"

But Lucía was already pulling off her goggles, an uncertain smile still tugging her lips. "Sorry, I just—"

Zuri waved off whatever she was going to say. "Believe me, I know my mother. You had no choice." She took a seat on the upholstered chair by the door and slipped off her shoes while she waited for her mother to lose. She knew Monique Hill would not simply *quit* out of a game, even if it was just a silly thing where you tried to place cables and generators to keep your fake town from having a fake blackout. Zuri wasn't into games, anyway, but she could not understand the attraction of this one in particular—balancing an electrical grid was hopelessly complex and a job for AI. This toy version was both silly and annoying. But her mother *loved* it.

Zuri sighed. Amani played it with her all the time. Zuri simply... couldn't. And she did not need another reminder of how she was failing at her relationships.

It was probably unprofessional for her to remove her shoes as well, but her feet were experiencing such blessed relief, she couldn't muster the energy to care.

Lucía had brought a chair to come sit by her. "How did it go?" She meant on the Island.

"No, no... dammit! You *bastard* bucket of rusty bolts!" Her mother was not a good loser.

Zuri ignored her. "Well, Miller is hiding something for sure."

Lucía nodded earnestly.

"That man is the slime on the bottom of barnacles." Her mother had slid off her goggles and was finger-combing out her tidy gray afro. Zuri was sure her large gold-hoop earrings were the same pair she'd had since she and Amani were babies, but her wrap-around tan sweater-top was the height of fashion. Her mother may be seventy, but Zuri hoped to look half as good at that age. Hell, she'd settle for having the zip in her mother's step *now*.

"You *barely* worked with Miller." Zuri scowled at her, annoyed for no reason.

"And yet, I know exactly the kind of man he is. I'm just tellin' the truth."

Zuri couldn't argue with that.

"Your mom worked on the Island with my parents!" Lucía gushed. "Well, not *with* my parents —she was in the fusion lab while they were in green tech. But I recognized your mom as soon as I walked in the door!" Lucía's eyes were full of that glow that Zuri's mother usually engendered in people half her age—less than half, in Lucía's case.

"They were lovely people," her mother said. "And you and your brothers, zipping all over the Island, getting into trouble. I was rooting for you, every time."

Lucía grinned. Her mother went on, explaining how Zuri and Amani stayed in school on the mainland with their father while she worked on the Island. Monique Hill had all the natural charisma that Amani seemed born with. Zuri used to say Amani got all the personality, and she got all the brains. Together, they made a complete human. But their mother had *both*—as did their father, who had been sharper than half of Hollywood put together. Somehow, Zuri ended up with only the brainy side: studious and serious, while Amani entertained and won hearts. Zuri was never jealous, not really. Amani was simply her other half, freeing her to be as nerdy as she wanted. Only now, that half was gone... and Zuri felt the sharp sting of it every time her mother looked at her.

Like something was missing. *Someone.*

There was a reason she hadn't visited this house much since the funeral, even though she lived practically next door.

Her mother was staring at Zuri right now, having taken a seat next to Lucía. Both were. Like she'd fuzzed out and missed a beat. Again.

Zuri pulled in a breath. "Well... Miller thinks Lucía is having some kind of mental breakdown."

"*What?*" Lucía's shock quickly turned to anger. "You can't... don't tell me you..." She was sputtering.

Her mother was peering at Zuri, head leaned

back and cocked, like she thought her daughter was the one with a mental breakdown. "I wouldn't believe a thing that man said."

"I know." She scowled at that extra suspicion. "Mama, I could use a minute alone with Lucía." Her mother scowled right back like she didn't quite trust Zuri. *"Please."* This was her fault, that things weren't right between them. Hadn't been since Amani died. And here she was throwing Lucía into her house to be taken care of. Not that her mother would mind, it just... *complicated* things. Things like why Zuri never came around anymore. Why she was avoiding all the family functions. Why she never talked about Amani, even though she was never more than a few thoughts away. And always in the mirror.

Her mother rose from her chair. "I'll just go fix some dinner for our guest."

Lucía watched the gigawatt charge between the two of them and kept quiet.

Zuri waited until her mother had gone into the kitchen and closed the door. "Sorry about that," she said to Lucía.

"I'm sorry I'm getting in the way here." There was genuine pain on the girl's face.

"It's not you, Ms. Ramirez." *Zuri* was the one who didn't belong, not anymore. Most of her life, it had been the three of them—Mama, Amani, and Zuri. When they were five years old, they marched by their mama's side for racial justice. During all their years growing up, their father was on set a lot, but the three of them were always together. Even when Zuri went to the Institute and Amani to USC, they still roomed together, off-campus, with a couch for Mama to come visit. Then there were the years Zuri worked on the Island with their mother. During that short time, Amani got into the business with their father, acting, doing her activism and her art. But then their father bought the Hillstead and moved everyone in, and it was like a fairy tale. One that got tarnished almost right away when he passed only a year later. That was nine years ago, and Zuri didn't think Mama would have survived if she hadn't had her girls. Both of them.

And now only one.

"Director Hill-Gray?" Lucía's voice was soft, her brown eyes round and concerned.

Shit. "It's been a long day. And you can call me Zuri."

Lucía nodded, but the concern on her face didn't lessen.

"Lucía, I need to ask you something, and I need you to be honest with me."

"All right."

Zuri envied the openness on Lucía's face—not naivete, just a calmness that said she'd seen some things, and whatever this was, she could handle it. *Confidence.* Zuri used to have it, but she'd lost her hold a year ago and hadn't found it since.

"Miller thinks you have some kind of grudge against Power Island One. On account of losing your family there."

Lucía's expression opened even more into pure surprise. "Um. Okay. That's... kind of crazy."

"That's what I thought. But I also know how hard it is to lose family. My father passed away nine years ago, and I still miss him every day. My twin sister died last year, and nothing's been the same since. I know how much that kind of loss shifts your entire world. So, if there's something more going on here, Lucía, I promise I'll understand. But I need to know what it is."

Lucía shook her head like she was clearing Miller's crazy out of her head. "It was strange at first to come back to the Island. But, believe me, I wanted nothing more than to settle in with my new family and make a home here. I *want* to work on the Island. It's all I've ever wanted. And this family I've found... they're the best. We've signed papers and everything. All I want is for whoever's doing this to just *stop*."

Zuri nodded. And she believed her. "Then we need to figure out what Miller is trying to hide. And who might be willing to kill to keep it secret."

Then Lucía stunned her by reaching across the space between their chairs and taking Zuri's hand. She squeezed it gently, reassuring. "I'm so sorry about your sister. I didn't know." Then she leaned back.

Zuri was so struck by it, she had no words at all.

Lucía filled the empty space of her non-reaction. "I've only known you a short time, Madam Director, but I know what it's like to carry that grief every day. You should know: it doesn't show." She gave a small smile. "I know how hard that is to pull off."

If Zuri didn't have words before, she didn't even have thoughts now. Lucía couldn't have stunned her more if she'd hit her with a baseball bat.

"Well. All right, then." As Zuri struggled to recover, her mother swept into the room with a tray of tea—it was her favorite wicker one with three steaming mugs hand-crafted by Auntie Vivian.

Lucía's eyes lit up.

"Chickpea stew's defrosting." Her mother handed out the mugs and took a seat again. "Where are we? Have we decided Miller's a stone-cold killer? Because I'll vote for that."

Lucía cradled her mug and blew on the tea. "Your mom's up to speed on everything."

"Of course, she is." Zuri reined in the emotional vortex set off by Lucía's simple compassion. Why had that hit her so hard? She focused instead on her mother. "What I can't figure is what this is all about. What's so important to go to all this trouble to cover up? What was Miller doing down in those old fusion labs?"

"And Casimir, the fake museum director." Lucía sipped her tea.

"Well, the obvious thing is *fusion*." Her mother set her tea on the side table and leaned forward, hands on her knees. "Now, you know how I feel about them shutting down those labs in 2040."

"You seemed to like the idea of moving to the Hillstead at the time," Zuri needled her, but it was gentle. That first year at the Hillstead was the last for her father, not that they knew it. If her mother and father hadn't both retired early to make the Hillstead happen, they wouldn't have had that last year together.

"The Hillstead was one thing," her mother

pushed back. "Shutting down those labs was simply a lack of imagination."

"And also funding." Zuri filled in Lucía on the missing details. "My mother retired from working the fusion labs when Energy Island was shut down and became Power Island One. The entire fusion staff either quit, retired, or got reassigned. I went into administration, which is how I eventually rose up to the Regional Director level." Back to her mother, she added, "Ellis was pretty damn disgruntled, as I recall. I overheard Miller mention him today—Astra, the power engineer working the VIV, is assisting Ellis on the project, whatever it is. They've got some kind of deadline they're trying to meet but need more data, according to Miller. I tried to lean on her to spill but didn't get very far."

Lucía was soaking it in. "The energy they were stealing from the mainland—all the outages—were powering a huge bank of batteries in the old lab space. That fits with fusion research."

"Maybe on the energy side," Zuri's mother said, "but you can't tell me Ellis was powering up a fusion reactor on the Island, and no one ever noticed. Never mind the power requirements, there's cooling. And those things are damn *loud*. Forget the pumps, the cooling, the raw power you're pumping in, just the reactor itself. That thing screams like a little child. Now maybe you wouldn't hear all that—we did insulate it and put it underground for a reason—but Ellis isn't running that by himself. Not even with this Casimir person and Astra to help. He'd need a lot more staff."

"And supplies," Zuri agreed. "Shielding, magnetic containment, compressed gases, hoses and clamps. And if he's got a new design he's tinkering with—tokamak, stellarator, or even something totally new—it would be really complex to build. That means engineers who understand how to put a toroid together and wire it up, not just a physicist with a grand plan."

"And even if they reached break-even on energy," her mother added, "which we'd already done two decades ago, by the way, the real challenge was always keeping containment long enough to scale up energy production. That's an engineering feat, not a science one. Which is why I think they were foolish to shut it all down." She leaned back, arms crossed now. "We could have had it in five years."

"That's what everyone's been saying... for the last thirty."

"What about the money?" Lucía asked, raptly following their back-and-forth.

"She's right," her mother said, leaning forward again. "Where's Ellis been getting the money for all this?"

"Where'd he get the money to lay an extra cable to the mainland?" Zuri asked, somewhat rhetorically. The three fell silent for a moment as it sunk in—the scope on this was huge. It seemed more and more implausible that Ellis had simply gone rogue and conducted his own clandestine fusion research.

"So, if it's not fusion," Lucía said quietly, "what is it?"

Zuri scowled and counted off the things they knew, one finger at a time. "Something with the energy to slice apart the VIV under a 200-foot column of water. Something worth laying a clandestine cable to the mainland and stealing a ton of power through unscheduled blackouts. Something an Island designer would take all kinds of risks to keep secret."

"Something worth killing for," Lucía added.

"Something involving the most famous retired fusion physicist in the world." Her mother swiped something up on her display. She flicked a connection to Lucía's and Zuri's displays so they could see her search. "What have you been up to, Ellis, you old codger?"

Which was funny, given Ellis was younger than her mother. As her search results popped up—and there wasn't much; it was like Ellis had dropped off the face of the earth for the last ten years—Zuri added, "He was our boss, not our friend. Not even yours."

"Mind your business," her mother said absently, but it made Zuri smile.

"Wait, who is this?" Lucía asked, tagging an old photo of Ellis standing with a group of scientists in front of a reactor. Looked like the one from Energy Island. He was probably forty-five in the picture, but he had to be at least sixty now. Younger than Monique by a decade but looking older, graying hair even at middle age. The last time Zuri saw him, his hair had gone completely white.

"That's the man himself," her mother said.

Zuri peered past the data at Lucía. "What's wrong?"

"That's *Casimir*." Lucía shook her head in disbelief. "I vaguely remember meeting Ellis when I was a kid on the Island, yet I didn't recognize him. Ellis *is* Casimir. He was literally down in the museum before the fire."

"Well, now we know he's in this for sure," Zuri said, returning to the search. "But I'm not seeing any publications or lab affiliations or research proposals from him since Energy Island shut down."

Her mother closed the link between the three of them. "That cable you're wondering about? The one to the mainland? All those were laid after the Island was towed into US waters. I wasn't involved in that operation. But you were in administration, Zuri. Could an extra cable have been put down at that time?"

Zuri nodded. "We contracted that work out. The Island staff was paring down, and everything was chaotic in those early days. Wouldn't have been too hard to pay off the contractor and slip that by the administration. No one was paying attention to what they did under the Island. Not until they started setting up the VIV."

"And if Ellis had no intention of actually stopping his research..." Her mother left that hanging.

"He would have planned ahead," Zuri finished. "Set it up so he could keep working."

Lucía frowned. "But all those labs were shut down during the conversion to Power Island One. The equipment moved out. Casimir—*Ellis*—made a point about how people were like vultures, making off with souvenirs."

Zuri nodded. "Yes, but the 'museum' was set up

to preserve most of it. I bet he held back the critical things. Or maybe brought in new equipment? Either way, this has been going on for ten years. At a minimum, Ellis planned for this from the beginning."

"Not the blackouts, though," Lucía said. "Those are new. At least, I think so."

Her mother wagged a finger at her. "Maybe it's not fusion. Maybe Ellis started a new, secret research program on the Island, and it's just now coming to fruition a decade later. Or they've entered a new phase of the testing."

"One that needed a lot of power." This was starting to make some sense to Zuri. "Okay, I'll need to track down *when* these outages started. Miller said one thing I agree with—the mainland grid balancing AI is under the Regional Director's purview. Which means, if someone's tampering with that, I should be able to track it down. I have someone in USEC who can help us with that. But she won't be in until Monday."

"Well, then that's settled." Her mother rose up. "Lucía will stay with us until Zuri tracks down these bastards and sends them to jail. Right?"

"Might not be that simple, Mama." But she hoped...

"I tell you what, your sister would be having a fit about this."

Zuri flinched. Because it was true, but also because while Zuri never went a day—sometimes an hour—without thinking about Amani, she never talked about that out loud. Not if she could help it. But her mother kept on as if Amani had just left the room and not their lives. There was a reason Zuri hardly ever came to visit.

"I appreciate you letting me stay here, Mrs. Hill." Lucía, bless her, was filling up the awkward silence.

A knock at the door preceded it swinging open. Grandaddy Terrell shuffled his wiry 85-year-old body through the doorway then stopped in surprise at seeing Lucía. "Oh! Didn't know you had company. I'll come back." He started backtracking.

"No, wait, Grandad." Zuri climbed out of the chair and slid her feet into her shoes. "I was just going." Terrell rambled around the Hillstead, poking in when it got to be about dinner time. "Monique's defrosting some chickpea stew."

"I do like that chickpea stew." Terrell smiled and eased back in, clearing the doorway.

"I'll message you later," Zuri tossed off to Lucía, who was already grinning at Terrell as he angled for the comfortable chair Zuri had just vacated. Zuri paused at the door, catching her mother's eye. "Thank you, Mama."

She waved her off. "You know where to find me." Then turned her attention to Terrell.

Zuri did—and she shouldn't stay away so much. Just as soon as she cleaned up this mess with work, she would do better. Her mama had only one daughter left. Zuri couldn't be Amani, much less both combined, but there was no excuse for acting like her mother had lost both. Even if it hurt.

She watched her mother usher Granddad and Lucía into the kitchen.

Then she hurried home to a husband and kids who likely thought she was a ghost as well.

FIVE

Bringing Lucía back to USEC felt like progress.

They'd gone over everything yesterday, again and again, and then twice more. Whatever had been happening in the old fusion labs, they knew the fire was a cover, nothing had been destroyed, just moved off-Island. The question was where? Whatever the project was, it was using energy, which had to come from somewhere. And someone had *already* manipulated the mainland grid AI to hide it. That might be the key. They had gotten nowhere searching online for Ellis. He'd gone completely off-grid.

It wasn't easy to disappear like that. Sure, digital privacy laws were famously strict, and you had nearly-complete control over public-facing records, but Digital Management Services required a minimum level of footprint for tracking. Short of court-ordered anonymity, you *existed* in some capacity online. Zuri had higher clearance than your average person for accessing semi-private records, but Ellis had gone dark after his fusion research had been shut down in 2040. To get scrubbed completely meant you were an anti-chipper living in a solar yurt with a sustenance farm... or you had powerful friends.

She knew Ellis—he would be the last man on Earth to go crunchy.

What was he trying so hard to hide?

Monday had finally rolled around, so she and Lucía were cruising through the security checks at the IEC in an attempt to find out. If they could track down when the outages started—or find anomalous energy usage in a new location—they'd have a chance to stop the power siphoning, and more important, blast open Ellis's secret. Then Lucía could go back to her normal life. Zuri as well, although her life was nothing like "normal" anymore. But enough time living in peace on the Hillstead might eventually heal what was broken inside her.

Zuri messaged ahead so Gwen would expect them.

USEC had a rather massive AI division, given how insanely complicated a job it was to manage power for the country. The parent organization, the IEC, was mainly political, much like the UN—an international intergovernmental organization that coordinated the race to zero carbon, facilitating money flowing into Energy Island initially and disseminating technology back out to the world once it was shut down. The Power Islands were still a huge source of ongoing technology development, so that arrangement still held—plus the IEC had evolved to broker agreements between countries about all aspects of the race to zero carbon. Emissions limits, petroleum quotas, carbon sequestration targets, and more. The IEC building in LA was like the UN building in NYC, only the players were arguably more powerful—ridding the globe of climate-driven pandemics was the full-time focus of nearly every nation on Earth. Given the WSO's Pandemic Corps was also headquartered in the IEC complex, LA was an international hub for managing the climate crisis.

For all that global effort concentrated in one location, USEC was more operationally focused. The National Director of USEC was the US liaison to the IEC, but State Directors and Regional Directors like Zuri were concerned primarily with the grid. USEC started out managing the US's conversion to a green energy economy. Not regulation of the electricity market—that was handled separately—but the transition itself. At first, that meant buildouts of the Power Islands, which USEC directly managed. Over time, that grew to mean coordination of the grid—leveraging the Island power sources, strategic management of the buildout of solar and wind across the country, both industrial farms and distributed consumer sources, and revamping the entire nationwide grid. Balancing the grid became a massive undertaking that quickly demanded a likewise massive AI system—or series of interconnected AI systems—to keep electricity sweeping across the country. Solar in the East would light up first, sending kilowatts to the still-dark West, and vice versa at the end of the day. Nationwide coordination and strategic infrastructure building, including industrial-scale battery storage, gained efficiencies at every turn. It wasn't enough to simply build a solar farm and store the energy. An AI system that could forecast need and dynamically match supply 24/7, every day of the year, became an absolute necessity. This was why USEC's computing department took up an entire wing of the IEC.

As Zuri and Lucía rode the elevator to the top floor, Zuri quickly checked her messages.

One from Jeevika said she'd cleared out Zuri's calendar. *I've postponed today's tentative meeting with the state regulators to tomorrow—there's a meeting prep in your folder. They're definitely responding to pressure from the protesters about the Palm Springs solar farms. I'm holding all your calls today. Last week's grid management data report is done processing and waiting for you, but there's no urgency to that. The <u>Q</u>uarterly Reviews for Power Islands Six through Twelve are scheduled for Wednesday. Should I postpone?*

Zuri quickly swiped back. *No. I'll catch up in time.* Once this business with Ellis and Miller got cleared out, she would plow through the reports. This was already taking up time and energy she didn't have, but she didn't get to be Regional Director without being able to handle multiple crises at once. Although the feeling this was *big*—like impossible-to-control big—had kept her up last night, tossing and twisting the sheets around her legs. She got up so she wouldn't wake Denzel, but that meant she was short on energy this morning.

"Who exactly are we meeting?" Lucía asked as they stepped out of the elevator.

"Her name's Gwen, and she's the most talented coder I have on staff."

Lucía nodded as they wove through a maze of cubicles to reach Gwen's office in the corner. Her spectacular view was blocked—she'd dialed down all the windows—and her office was nearly dark. Her door nameplate said, *Gwen Della, Not Her Real Name.* Zuri peered through the glass sidelight that flanked the door. Gwen sat in a high-backed chair, facing away from them, hands working the air. Her desk to the right had a dozen screens mounted on the wall and was littered with her usual personal effects.

"She's probably in virtual," Zuri said before she knocked lightly and opened the door. "Hey, Gwen," she called, hoping the woman didn't have mute plugs.

"Hey, Z!" Gwen spun her chair around, lifted her goggles to her forehead, then jazzed her hands above her head in greeting. Then surprise popped on her face. "Whoa, your hair got big! How long has it been?"

"A while." Zuri smiled but then froze as Gwen leaped out of her chair, strode across the room, and threw her arms around Zuri.

"I'm so sorry about Amani." Gwen's hug was intense, way too long, and this skinny little white girl was *strong*—Zuri could hardly breathe under the assault. Gwen held on until Zuri awkwardly hugged her back.

Lucía's eyes were wide.

Not that Zuri minded—it was just that Gwen had been Amani's friend first, doing all their protests and activism together. Zuri was the occasional tag-along, and that ended when Amani died. Zuri was also Gwen's boss, three levels above, but that didn't matter.

Gwen sighed and finally released her. "Still can't believe she's gone." Then she seemed surprised to find Lucía next to her just inside the doorway. "Hold up! Who's your *very* conventionally attractive friend, Z?"

"This is Lucía Ramirez." Zuri was still recovering from the hug. "She's one of my power engineers."

Gwen stepped back and performed an elaborate bow, touching her forehead and waving her hand. It made Lucía erupt in a strangled laugh, and that somehow cut the tension holding Zuri's shoulders taut. She motioned Lucía farther into the room then closed the door.

"We've got a problem," Zuri started.

"Don't we all?" Gwen backed into her seat, plopping down with enough energy to make it roll, then snagged a pair of drumsticks off her desk and drummed the air as she spoke. "Let me guess: corporate hacks want to jack up rates on the poor, and you want me to spoof their chips and blackmail them with their own dick pics." She punctuated that with a rap-tap on her desk with the drumsticks.

"No." Zuri gave her a look, but it had no effect.

"Okay, second guess: rare earth miners are using slave labor again, and you want me to crowd-source shorting their stocks?" Another beat on the desk to round it out.

"*Gwen.*"

"What? I could totally do that for you."

"I know." It was the kind of thing Gwen and Amani would dream up one weekend and implement the next. Gwen's desk was filled with pictures of her at protests—*Synth Milk Feels No Pain*—along with pictures of her cat Karl and her band, *The Angry Hats.* "I need your help to stop someone siphoning power from the grid."

She stopped air-drumming and sat straight up in her chair. "Well, that's... new." She frowned. "The AI would identify and spit that out like a bad grape. But you're coming to me with this, which means this isn't kids trying to steal some juice for their secret weed farm bot. Is it? Because that would be sizzling. Not sure I could engage in activities that might dampen that kind of enthusiastic takedown of the Deep Electric in which I am otherwise gainfully employed."

At least Zuri had her attention. "This is much worse."

"Aight. Tell me." Gwen set her drumsticks down.

Zuri nodded to Lucía, who flicked a file they'd prepared over to Gwen. "This is all the information we've got," Lucía said. "There's a secret power cable that's been laid between the mainland and Power Island One. Someone used it to draw down power from the mainland through rolling blackouts that also did a rapid draw-down on residential batteries and destroyed them. Someone's using this power for a secret project—we don't know what, but there have been multiple, severe, and escalating attempts to cover it up. When we got close, they shut down the operation and moved it. We want to track when the previous outages started and see if we can find any new anomalous power usage that might pinpoint where they moved to."

Gwen was furiously paging through the documents Lucía sent. "Okay, kids. This is some serious shit." Gwen pulled her gaze from her display and looked to Zuri. "I like her, by the way." She flashed a smile at Lucía then spun toward her desk. "Let's see what we can dig up on these electron thieves." Half her bank of screens lit up with the documents they'd provided, the other half with real-time analysis of the grid. Gwen's official job was fine-tuning and monitoring one of the AI subsystems that tracked and predicted usage in several industrial sectors throughout the greater LA metro area. She was well-versed in finding deviations from normal grid operation as well as the AI systems that kept them all running.

"What's our target date range on these nefarious outages?" Gwen asked.

"The last one was a week ago—my new family says it's been going on for months, at least."

"New family, huh?" Gwen asked, her fingers flying over a virtual keyboard she'd summoned. "Did ya' get married or something?"

"No." Lucía lifted an eyebrow at Gwen.

"Boyfriend?" Gwen peeked up. "Girlfriend?"

Zuri poked her in the back. "Don't make me report you to HR. And can we *focus* here?"

"I can multitask." She shot another flirtatious smile to Lucía, who seemed to be taking it rather good-naturedly. "Also, pretty sure this doesn't fall under any category of *work* to which I've been assigned."

"*Gwen.*" Zuri wasn't as good at the banter as Amani had always been.

"Not that that ever stopped me," Gwen said absently, but something on one of the screens had caught her attention. "Well, this is fucked up."

"What is it?" Zuri leaned in, taking a closer look at the spectrum analysis Gwen had scrolling by, but she had no reference for what it was.

Gwen swiped it away, and her hands moved even faster as she explained. "Okay, the weirdness here is that the AI should have adapted—compensated for anyone hacking into the grid *wherever* and draining juice."

"That's what I thought," Lucía said. "That they had to have retargeted the AI somehow."

"Right you were, cute stuff." But Gwen's frown was getting darker. "And let me tell you exactly how much it *pisses me off* to have people tampering with the grid's AI." She gritted her teeth and slid a look to Zuri. "A *lot* of piss-off-edness." Then back to the screen, which was populating out a map of LA with a series of dots. "But not quite as much as *this* fuckery."

Lucía and Zuri both leaned in to examine it.

Clusters of dots flared up, red then blue then orange... then back to red, but shifted to a new section of the map.

"This is just going back six months," Gwen explained. "These are anomalous outages that were somehow targeted intentionally by the AI, draining power from these microgrid locations to something called Power Station 76. Only there's no Power Station 76, so that's your bleed via secret cable out to Power Island One. Notice anything about the location of these dots?"

Zuri didn't.

Lucía pointed to one cluster at a spot about a mile inland from Huntington Beach. "That's my family's cottage. They've been hit for a while."

"That's one of the more upscale neighborhoods." Gwen's voice had dropped to anger mode. "Most of these are in poorer neighborhoods. Refugee centers. Low-income housing. The City of Homes, largest site of transitional housing in LA. There are at least 10,000 people in that village. In other words, people with no political power to complain and who can get denied basic services without much danger of being found out." Gwen pushed back from her desk, folded her arms across her chest, and leveled her gaze at

Zuri. "I don't like these guys. How do we destroy them?"

"We have to figure out where they are now." Zuri already thought she'd have to go back to Astra. *They had proof now.* Something solid she could use to pressure Astra into flipping on Miller.

Gwen turned back to her screens and her virtual keyboard. "The most recent incident was a week ago, which tracks with your on-the-ground observation of when the outages stopped. I'm widening my search, tapping into the neighboring grids outside the LA Basin…"

"How could this not show up on any of your system checks?" Lucía asked, then looked sheepish. "No offense, it just seems…"

"Amateurish? Clown town? Like we don't know what the fuck we're doing?" Gwen spat out the words one at a time. Then she peeked up at Lucía. "I'm not mad at you. That's exactly what it looks like. Which is galling because our system has *values programming*. It has specific system checks to make sure there are no adverse impacts of any kind on vulnerable communities. I was part of that committee, for fuck's sake. Whoever hacked us is making a mockery of that. And they're *good*. I have no idea how they got in, but you can bet your buttons, I'm gonna find out. Who knows what else they've fucked with. Are *still* fucking with. This is a disaster."

"Right now, we need to know where they are," Zuri said.

"Working on it."

Zuri was internally debating if she should just punch out, leave Lucía here to monitor progress, and go after Astra immediately. Before this got any more out of hand. But this was a relief. If the anomalies were invisible to Gwen—to the entire system of internal checks at USEC's AI department—then it wasn't Zuri's fault. She would take responsibility for anything that happened on her watch, but her deepest fear was that it would be something *she personally* had messed up. But no matter how checked-out she might have been this last year, lost in the vortex of losing Amani, it was a relief to know this wasn't something she should have caught. Which didn't make it any less of a disaster, but she was on it now. And the magnitude of this assault was just settling in. She was quickly reaching the *royally pissed off* level of outrage where Gwen had set up camp.

Before Zuri could decide whether to head out to Power Island One again, an alert popped up on her display. Bright red with an audible screech a half-second behind it. *What...?*

"What is this?" Gwen paused her urgent searching to swipe at her display.

"Oh, shit." Lucía had it too.

Power outages. All over the LA Basin. "What the hell is happening?" Zuri flipped furiously through her display. A cascade failure was sweeping across the city.

"Shit. Shit. *Shit.*" Gwen was stabbing at her display. Then she swung to Zuri and their gazes locked. "They know we found them."

Zuri choked. "Are you sure?"

"No. Not 100%. But Zuri... *get out of here.* You do *not* want to be here right now."

"What do you mean? I'm not going anywhere."

Lucía was already at the door. "She means out of the computing department. They'll try to pin this on you."

"*What?*" Zuri's mind was reeling.

"Go!" Gwen waved frantically at Lucía. "Get her out of here."

"*Madam Director,*" Lucía begged.

Zuri hesitated, frozen... then went with Lucía as she hustled out the door.

SIX

Zuri was hiding in her executive bathroom.

Hiding probably wasn't the right word—she'd legitimately needed to use the facilities—but now she stood, hyperventilating at the sink, hand pressed to the mirror... and she couldn't move. A face she barely recognized stared back at her. Eyes wide. Lips parted and gasping. A flush in her cheeks which darkened them even further. She had Amani's hair, but the rest was pure, panicked Zuri.

"Breathe," she commanded her reflection. Then she closed her eyes and obeyed. One breath, two, three. A half dozen before it felt safe to open them again. "You can do this." The determination in her eyes brought Amani back to the mirror. The fiery passion she always had, especially for things like this.

Injustice. Corruption. Amani would be clamoring for investigations and indictments, no matter how long the odds. *Compassion isn't being nice,* she would say. *It's fighting like hell for the people who would get trampled otherwise.*

Zuri was doing that—the grid's AI was compromised, but that didn't mean there weren't backstops. Ways to manually reroute and restore power, which were seldom used, only in extreme events which lay outside the AI's ability to predict and manage. Zuri had quickly gotten authorization to bring backup supplies online, then managed the scramble to identify each and every outage and get it restored as quickly as possible.

When she'd finally taken a break to use the restroom, they were back to 95% power restored, with the average outage only fifteen minutes long. Still enough to incite a hell of a lot of panic. And that left a million people without power in small pockets around the 20 million households and businesses in the greater Los Angeles Metro area.

An audio-only call from Jeevika buzzed her display.

Zuri pulled in a breath and flicked to answer it.

Her assistant jumped in without preamble. "I've got Governor Kipo'mo on the line, Zuri. How are you holding up? Should I tell her you're still working the situation?" Jeevika had been managing the flood of calls, everyone from LA Mayor Booker Johnson to the Chairman of the state Public Utility Commission wanting an update on the "situation."

"No, put her through."

"You okay?" Jeevika checked again.

"Not really."

"Putting her through."

Zuri waited until Kirsten Kipo'mo's serious portrait flashed upon her display. Southern California's first indigenous governor was known for her straight talk, so Zuri kept to the facts. "Governor Kipo'mo, thank you for calling. We've got 95% containment here in the LA Basin—my people tell me we'll have the last 5% within a half-hour."

"Containment of *what*, Director Hill-Gray?"

"That's what we're figuring out, ma'am. Right now, we're focused on restoring power, but I promise: you'll have a full report as soon as we diagnose the situation." Zuri rubbed her forehead and checked the mirror—and gave thanks the governor hadn't insisted on a face-to-face video call. She was a wreck.

"I'll want more than a report. I want to see an action plan on how USEC will prevent this from ever happening again. Our citizens rely on our power

—and the pact we've made with them to provide it. *Reliably,* Director Hill-Gray."

"Understood." This catastrophic breakdown had broken every trust agreement between USEC and the public—that in exchange for nearly complete control over the grid, USEC would maintain a reliable, cost-effective, efficiently-used, low-carbon power supply to the people. It wasn't so much that a short power outage was catastrophic—it was that the trust the whole agreement rested on was fragile. *That* was what Zuri had to restore, in a hurry.

The governor hung up without saying anything more. Zuri let out a breath in relief.

Hiding in the bathroom wouldn't help.

Zuri straightened her clothes, gave herself a stern look in the mirror, and headed back out to her office. Lucía was coordinating the effort to restore power— she was on virtual with three departments, tracking down the outages, rerouting power around compromised substations, and pulling power from residential backup systems. Ironically, they were using methods not far different from Miller's illicit project: they were reversing the flow and pulling power from backups, both home and electric vehicle batteries, all over the LA Basin. The difference was that USEC was doing it *responsibly* and not damaging people's systems. And also, this was a legitimate power usage, not whatever the fuck Miller had going. Or Ellis. Whoever was orchestrating this.

"How are we doing?" Zuri asked, then leaned against her desk. Her shoulders felt like they were holding up the entire IEC building.

"Back up to 98%." Lucía's hands were manipulating the air in front of her. "Gwen still hasn't found a way to block our saboteurs, or where the new power drains might be, but they seem to have only staged a single attack—draining backups in a scattershot of communities all over the region in one shot. She's still tracking where the power *went*."

"How long until we're back to 100%?"

"Fifteen minutes. Give or take." Lucía flicked a look to Zuri. "I can't even imagine the heat you're getting for this."

Zuri just nodded. She could wait 15 minutes, until she had good news to report, before returning all these calls. The Mayor. USEC's state director for Southern California. Every single commissioner on the state's Public Utility Commission. She might just call the Chairman. Even the RTO—Regional Transmission Organization—office had lit up her chip. She'd probably be answering to FERC by the end of the day. The Federal Electric Regulatory Commission was hands-off, but they were the most direct oversight in the chain-of-command for USEC, ever since USEC absorbed all the responsibilities of FERC's operational underling, NERC. The Northern American Electric Reliability Corporation used to oversee the grid, maintaining a steady source of power for the country back when it was mostly supplied by fossil fuels. Then in 2028, when the Energy Island project kicked off, and USEC came into existence, the responsibility for transitioning the country off its fossil fuel habit and onto a clean, green energy one gradually was taken over by USEC. Ten years ago, when fusion research was shut down, NERC was officially disbanded. USEC took over all its responsibilities for maintaining grid reliability. USEC managed the Power Islands directly, and the rest of the mainland power suppliers indirectly—each of those had their own local, non-profit Public Utility that was customer-facing—but the overall grid management, and the AI system that made it possible, were the backbone of USEC.

A backbone that just had a terrible virus invade it.

"Back at 100%!" Lucía enthused.

Zuri checked the time—not even 15 minutes.

"Tell Gwen I owe her several bottles of that terrible tequila she likes."

Lucía grinned and typed away, probably relaying that message immediately.

"And I need a report on everything that was down, all our mitigation strategies, and a full inventory of complaints this spooled up for us," Zuri added. "Everything except where this came from. I'll need to put together a coherent story on that separately."

Lucía got busy and was a life-saver in this crisis. Zuri should consider her for an administrative role in USEC, if she was even interested. Power Engineers tended to want to do just what Lucía was doing today: get elbows deep in the power system and fix it. Or keep it running. They were problem-solvers, but she sure could use more of those.

Zuri pulled in a deep breath and contemplated who she should call first. She fired off a message to Jeevika so she could reassure people. *Back at 100%. Will be returning my calls shortly.* Then a message flagged urgent came in but from an anonymous caller.

It simply said *Mainland grid management is the province of the Regional Director.*

The fuck? Was this someone's idea of a joke?

Someone with access to her messaging system but able to remain anonymous.

A chill was already seeping into her stomach before the next message came through.

Back off. Take responsibility. Twelve hours or it will happen again.

Oh... shit.

"Gwen says that tequila is not a sufficient reward," Lucía said cheerily. "She demands fair-trade premium vodka." Then her face fell. "Madam Director?"

"It's Miller." Her voice was soft. The horror had muted everything. "He's saying he'll do it again. If we don't back off."

Lucía's expression fell blank. "He can't... that's..."

"Holding the entire Los Angeles Metro area hostage? Yes. That's exactly what he's doing." She touched her fingertips to her forehead just to make sure her head was still attached. It felt like it was floating away.

"But... he can't do that!" Lucía protested again.

Zuri shook her head. She felt dizzy. "He was willing to kill you, Ms. Ramirez. He wouldn't hesitate to cut off power to millions. Repeatedly. Randomly." It was getting hard to breathe. "He'd do it until I was hounded out of USEC. Disgraced." She blinked and found Lucía staring at her, horrified. "And who would listen to me then about some crazy secret project siphoning power from the grid?"

If she took responsibility for this, blamed it on some USEC failing, not an external hack, like Miller wanted, that would end her career. Either way, Miller would win. And if she didn't do what he wanted, millions would suffer.

It was a box with no escape.

"You can't... just... let him get away with this." Lucía was shaking her head in tiny motions.

"We're at 100%, right?" She was blinking too much, peering at Lucía like her eyes couldn't focus.

"Yes, but—"

"Tell my assistant to hold all my calls. I'm... leaving."

"What?" Lucía just stared at her as she lumbered toward the door of her office.

She stopped there, hand on the knob, frozen for a moment. Then she looked back to Lucía. "You can go home now. He's not after you anymore."

Then she turned and walked out of her office.

———

Zuri honestly didn't remember the ride home.

One minute she was hailing an autocar outside the IEC complex, the next she was climbing out and staggering down the walking path of the Hillstead like she was drunk. The sun blazed overhead. Somehow it was bright and shining out when her whole world had actually gone dark. She'd literally turned her chip off when she left the office, which she *never* did. She passed her mother's house, kept on down the path, head down, determined to make it home before she collapsed. And what then? She didn't even know.

It was all over.

"Zuri? Child, you're back!"

She stopped without meaning to. Auntie Vivian stood in her open doorway, waving at her. For a moment, Zuri just stared. It was like her brain couldn't make sense of what Vivian was saying.

Then Cora appeared at the door, behind her wife. "What's wrong with her?"

"I can hear you," Zuri said, although she had missed something, obviously.

"There's nothing wrong with her." But Auntie Vivian was leaving her porch now, coming to collect up Zuri, an arm looped around hers and towing her back into their house.

"I need to go home." But Zuri couldn't muster the energy for much protest.

"Sure, you do," Auntie Vivian said, guiding her to the kitchen table. "But you can stop over for a minute."

Zuri was legitimately mystified *why*.

"She has a new recipe," Cora explained as she settled at the other end of the table. The electronic parts for her painting bot, the one she was building to help train the refugees in Vivian's arts project, were arranged on the table, mid-assembly. Several of Vivian's latest paintings were hung around the dining table, on easels or the wall. "It's got honey, Jojoba oil, something called guar gum, and... something else."

"Rosemary oil." Vivian reappeared from the back bathroom with a cape, a spray bottle, and a small ceramic bowl. "We haven't conditioned your hair in so long, I figure it's just what you need to pick up your spirits. And this recipe is guaranteed to banish that frizz and those dry ends and just bring back that shiny." She set the bowl on the table then swirled the cape around Zuri.

"Vivian, I don't—"

"Hush. This won't take but a minute." She tucked the cape into the collar of Zuri's blouse.

"Then it sets in for twenty minutes, you get on back home, rinse it with cold water, and you tell Auntie Vivian if it doesn't perform the magic." She wetted down Zuri's hair with the spray bottle.

Cora just shrugged, like, *What can you do?* But then she peered at Zuri. "What's wrong? That mystery at Power Island One got you worried?"

"You didn't hear the news?" Zuri's voice was weak.

Vivian worked the conditioner from her bowl into Zuri's hair. "What news?"

"All the power outages? You didn't hear anything?" Zuri just blinked. It was like the Hillstead was its own island untouched by anything from the outside world.

"Honey, we don't read the news all that often," Vivian explained as she massaged Zuri's scalp then worked the conditioner down to the ends. "It's so depressing."

"You're the Regional Director," Cora said as she idly rearranged her bot parts on the table. "Isn't that your job, scheduling the outages?"

"Yes." And then the weight of everything just crushed her. She sat there, mute, letting Vivian work her hair and allowing the tears to just fall.

"Oh, hey, now..." Cora got up from her chair and

lurched over to Zuri's side. "I didn't mean it was your fault, honey."

"What did you *say?*" Vivian demanded of Cora, peering at Zuri's face, now streaked with tears.

"I don't know!" Cora's grimace and Vivian's fluster had no impact.

Zuri just silently wept tears she couldn't explain. Tears long coming, she supposed. It wasn't like she hadn't cried over Amani before, but these felt like ancient tears, welled up from a deep, dark cistern where they'd be waiting millennia for just the right pressure to shove them to the surface. They came and came, a new uncorked stream emptying her out.

Vivian and Cora kept quiet. Cora hustled off into the kitchen behind her. Vivian disappeared and returned quickly with a hot, steaming towel she wrapped all around Zuri's head, tucking it under and then securing it with a plastic cap. Cora returned with tea for all three, setting the mugs on the table as she and Vivian took seats on either side and stared anxiously at Zuri.

She couldn't begin to explain all that had happened.

"Without Amani, it's like there's only half of me." Vivian and Cora were glued to her, but she couldn't look at them, so she stared at the mug steaming before her. "Like there's a whole other side of me that's missing, and I keep waiting for it to come back." She met Vivian's concerned gaze. "The half that's still here is work. The Islands. The grid. All the meetings and reports and keeping all of it running. And now... I'm going to lose that too. And if that happens, Auntie..." The tears burned fresh. "I'm not sure what'll be left."

"Oh, baby." Vivian got up from her chair and wrapped her in a hug. Her roundish body was all softness and warmth. Zuri leaned into her, mindful of her hair all freshly wrapped up. She didn't want to undo Vivian's kindness, but she was out of every kind of steam.

Cora edged closer in her chair, found Zuri's hand, and gripped it. "Who's doing this, Zuri? Who's saying you're going to lose that big job of yours? 'Cuz I want to give them a piece of my mind. And possibly my fist."

Zuri squeezed her hand back. "You can't fix this, Cora."

"I wouldn't be so sure about that."

Vivian loosened her enveloping hug and tugged her chair closer so she could sit. "Baby, you haven't lost everything. No matter what's going on with that job of yours—and I know you love it—but that's not all there is. I know sometimes it can feel that way, though. Sometimes we lose things, like our sweet child Amani, and it feels like the entire world is gone. Swallowed up whole by the emptiness left behind. But it's not true. As long as you're still pulling in breath, you still have options. Choices."

Zuri watched her Auntie's lips as she spoke—she couldn't look her in the eyes—but the words were reaching across that space between them. They were working their way into her and taking hold.

"I do have a choice I have to make." It seemed like there was no winning answer, but it was still a choice.

"Sure you do." Vivian nodded. "And *you* get to decide the kind of person you want to be. The one who makes this choice or that. That's all we are, really, in the end. The kind of person who makes this choice or that."

Zuri frowned. But Vivian's words gave her a lifeline to the future. All this time, she'd been living in suspended animation. Waiting for the pain to stop. Waiting for Amani to fade from her window reflection... or maybe come back to life in the mirror, her own hair grown into a perfect replica. But the world kept marching on, and now she had to make a choice about this crazy thing Miller had done. Whatever it was, he was forcing her to take some kind of action, and that choice would define who she was—who her future self would be—for better and worse.

In a strange way, it was a chance to start over. To become someone new.

Zuri hugged Vivian, who wrapped her up again and almost didn't let go. Then she hugged Cora, which was a more awkward thing. Then she wiped her face and got a repeat of the instructions for her hair, so she'd do that right. She left her Aunties' house almost light-headed, floating out the door and down the walk toward her home, her husband, and her kids.

The kind of person she wanted to be.

Which choice would that be?

Now that her head was clearing, it seemed there had to be more options than simply caving in to Miller's demands or suffering the consequences. A third choice, although she didn't know what at that moment.

She opened the door to her house to the smell of something cooking in the kitchen—it boggled her mind that it was only lunchtime. Denzel must be making something for the kids. She shed her earrings and shoes by the door, but she didn't get three steps in before a pounding of bare feet—large ones—came hurrying toward her.

Denzel rounded the corner, eyes wide. "Zuri! Oh my God." He grabbed hold of her shoulders and gave her a furious looking over. "Are you all right?"

"What? I'm fine—"

He grabbed her into a hug. *"Holy shit,* you scared me."

"D, what in the world?" Then she didn't hear any small voices or bodies or feet. "Where are the kids? Is everything all right?"

He released her, still looking freaked. "They're at Nan's. The outages, Z! They're all over the news. You weren't answering any calls or messages. Jeevika said you weren't taking any calls. Lucía said you'd left the office. No one knew where you were..." He was in a state.

"Oh, baby, I'm sorry." She reached up to hug him again. "I just turned off my chip. Needed space to think." She pulled back. "Things are... bad."

Something was starting to smell *over*-cooked. "The eggs!" He dashed back to the kitchen, and by the time she got there, he was scraping them out of the pan, trying to rescue them. But he quickly set that aside and pulled a chair over where she'd taken a seat at the island counter. "All right, what is going on? Tell me everything."

She pulled in a breath. This wasn't just her decision. Whatever she did—however she chose to go with this—Denzel and the kids would be affected. Everyone on the Hillstead to some extent. "Miller's hacked the grid's AI somehow—we don't know how, and we can't stop him. At least, we haven't figured out how yet. He triggered the cascade of outages, pulling out a massive amount of power, just like before, only this time concentrated all at once. And he's threatening me, D. He's saying I have to back off, stop trying to look into what he's been doing on Power Island One."

"Or what?" Denzel's sweet face was wrinkled up in horror.

"Or he'll do it again. And I'm sure he won't stop until he ruins me—not to mention putting millions of people at risk by cutting off their power. He wants me to take the fall for the outage. And to stop the investigation. Or he'll force me to."

"That's no choice at all." Denzel's fist curled up on the counter. Her man didn't get violent—he had the softest touch of any person she knew. But he was trembling, and it broke her heart to see him afraid for her. Or maybe angry with nowhere to go with it.

She laid a hand on his fist. "I don't have any *good* choices. But I still have a choice."

He relaxed a little. "What are you thinkin'?"

She smiled, although it was hard. "About what Amani would do if she were here."

Her dear, sweet husband's expression just opened up, and she could see his kind heart—the one she fell in love with—in those deep eyes of his. "You don't have to be your sister, baby."

"Maybe I do." He frowned, so she hurried up the rest, even though it was still half-formed in her head. "I carry her in me anyway. All the time. Every time I look in the mirror, she's there, reminding me who she was—who *I* was when we still had her. It's like she's living in me. I'm her legacy, D. I carry *us* forward. So, what would Amani do with this hot mess Miller has given us?"

A slow smile was growing on her husband's face. "Probably tell him to fuck off."

"Yes, she would." The smile on Zuri's face was real and felt good. It brought tears with it, and that was okay, too. "She would say, *Oh, hell no, we're not letting some asshole steal power from everyone!*" She was fully in Amani-voice now, that righteous indignation her sister had when fired up. "Then she'd go get in Miller's face and probably have to be hauled out by security."

"Okay, I wouldn't recommend that part." His smile dimmed. "Millions of people without power... I know you can't let that happen."

"No." That part she was sure of. "And if I take the fall for this, make up some story about this catastrophic breakdown of the AI, say it was some failure on my watch, I'd probably lose my job. Which wouldn't be the end of things for us personally—we've got what we need here at the Hillstead—but it would be a lot harder to stop Miller from whatever he's doing if I'm not the Regional Director of USEC-LA any longer."

He nodded, slowly. "There's got to be someone you can go to with this."

She grimaced. "This thing is deep inside USEC. There are only a few people I can trust. And Miller only gave me twelve hours to come up with my story. If he thinks I'm hesitating or trying some shenanigans, I'm sure he'd trigger another set of outages to convince me. What I need is to figure out where he's moved his whole operation, maybe stop him there. And I need to shut down this hack he's managed into the AI. I'm sure Gwen's still working on that—or at least trying to block him—but as long as he has that, he can do as he likes. Even if Miller destroys my career, I can't let him have that kind of power over the next person. Or simply the ability to shut off the grid to all of LA. He's too dangerous a man to have that much power in his hands. And while I'm doing all *that,* I need to at least make him think he's won. Or he will crash things before the twelve hours are up."

Denzel was soaking up every word. "How are you going to do that?"

"I don't know. Channel some of Amani's acting talent, I suppose." She touched her wrapped up hair. "The Aunties gave me a gift."

"A new hair treatment?" He smiled at the change in subject.

"A new perspective. Now I need to see what I can do with it."

That brought a smile—a good one—to her husband's face. Then he kissed her in that way he had, where she was the whole of his universe, and for the first time in way too damn long, he had her entire attention for a spell.

SEVEN

"How long has it been since you've worn one of these?" Lucía asked.

Zuri zipped up the front of her standard Island-issued coveralls. "Way too long." She smiled a little. The nametag said *Jeremy*. "I don't think this is going to fool anyone, though."

"Good thing you're an official USEC employee, then."

"For the moment."

The afternoon was a blur. A frantic reconnection with Denzel in the shower had been followed up with turning her chip back on and hurrying back into the city. She'd briefed Jeevika, gotten updates from Gwen, and joined up with Lucía at the harbor, all while strategizing a plan to stop Miller before the clock ran out at ten that evening. That was twelve hours from his anonymous-but-clear message, although she couldn't be sure if he'd hold to that timeline. They would need every minute.

They'd made it to the Island by private charter, but Lucía recommended stopping at her apartment to change into work clothes. Zuri would stand out too much in her office wear, and her heels were ill-suited for the Island, but most important, they needed to reach Astra without tipping off Miller. According to the Island locator, she was in her apartment, and Miller wasn't on-Island, but if he could do half the things he'd done already, he could mask his presence. And if he caught wind of their plans, he might move up the timeline and cut power to millions of people before they could get Astra to flip on him.

Or tell them how he hacked the AI.

An incoming call from Gwen flashed in Zuri's peripheral vision. "Hang on," she said to Lucía, who was halfway to the door of her tiny, renovated garden shack. "Let's see what Gwen's got for us." It was a video call request, so Zuri slid her base station from her pocket and held it up so she'd be on camera. Then she swiped to accept the call. "Hey. We're about to go in. Unless you've got Miller locked out?"

"No luck yet on that." Gwen's face was haggard from chasing code all afternoon. She'd brought in a whole team who could be trusted to hunt down Miller's back door, but Zuri knew they had little to go on. It was one thing to trace power flows that had already happened—it was something different to detangle the AI to discover how someone *outside* the system could be influencing its self-learning behavior. "But I have something else for you."

"What's that?" Zuri flicked a mirror of the call to Lucía, so she could see and hear this as well.

"I think I've tracked where Miller sent all those kilowatts he drained this afternoon." Gwen sent a side message with a map of the LA Metro area, only it extended out to half the state. "I had to expand my search to the neighboring grids. By the way, I think that might be how he's getting in—the interfaces between the grids are hella complicated and might be encoding some signals we've not quite deciphered yet. But anyway, check this out." The LA portion of the grid lit up with a firecracker explosion of blue dots. "These are this morning's outages." Then a wave across dozens of power lines pulsed eastward and to the south, across LA and dumping into the Inland Empire grid. "That surge shorted out a whole bunch of secondary transfer stations."

"There are only a few lines that are meant to carry that kind of load," Zuri said.

"Right. And our buddy Miller was greedy. Or maybe just showboating. But he drew down more than he could carry. Then again, maybe he knew he'd have losses along the way."

"So where did it end up?"

"That's the crazy part." The map shifted farther east and south, into the desert. "The pulse left the LA area, ripped across the Inland Empire, funneled down to a narrow band near fucking Yucaipa of all places, and then just... disappeared."

"Did it blow something out?" Zuri asked. "Get dumped to ground?"

"That's what I thought, so I pulled in a friend I trust who works the Inland grid, and they had a friend who had a friend who moonlights as an unlicensed electrician... *anyway,* what's important is I got eyes on the ground, and you're not going to believe this. There's a ghost line strung with the main high-voltage lines that snake through that valley, hugging the mountains. It's not on any of the grid maps. And get this: it runs all the way to Palm Springs and dumps into the huge solar complex out there. It had to totally reverse the flow on that for a good two minutes. I have no idea how it didn't fry everything.

Maybe it did. My dude on the ground obviously couldn't get into the facility."

"That's the Renew Energy development." Zuri's mind was pinging.

"If you say so." Gwen rubbed her eyes and yawned. "Okay, I'm back to pulling spaghetti out of the AI. Let me know if you crack Astra like the nut she is and get something useful."

"Will do."

Gwen's call ended, but Lucía's eyes were lit up. "You think that's where Miller moved the project?"

"It would make sense." Zuri swiped the air to place an audio call to Jeevika, which she seldom did —they almost always messaged.

Which was why Jeevika sounded alarmed when answered. "Oh, hey, Boss. Everything okay down there?" Living in Toronto was giving her assistant's Indian English a Canadian accent. It was delightful.

Zuri jumped right to business. "Gwen says Palm Springs may be where Miller sent all that power from the outages."

"Whoa, really?"

"Right? Isn't that where the protests are right now?"

"Yeah. That's a strange coincidence."

"Get me up to speed on that."

"Right. Let me pull that up." Jeevika messaged a screen with images of the massive solar plant Renew Energy had in Palm Springs, as well as a bunch of text, but she walked Zuri through the highlights. "Renew Energy is petitioning the commissioners for another expansion—it's the third one this year. They're building out like crazy. The bulk of the protesters are residents, although there are the usual environmental activists joining in as the protest grows. They're going on four days now of continuous occupation outside the Palm Springs Solar Complex."

"Is it just the usual? Or is there something special about this expansion they're protesting?"

"As far as I can tell, it's a normal protest. Palm Springs has been ravaged. Deadly high heat days, up to 125 degrees F, are a constant risk, April through September. The economy has been in a steady decline for a decade, and while Renew brings in new jobs, the solar array itself is a heat island that's eating up neighborhood after neighborhood. Residents fear they're being pushed out by a facility that makes power, not for them, but for the city bleeding energy out of the desert. Palm Springs used to be a luxury resort, back before the climate devastation, so it's not like they're building on sacred lands. No indigenous protesters. No ecological protesters. EPA says no issues with endangered species like desert tortoise or ironwood tree stands. Bureau of Land Management says it's all built on previously disturbed lands. But there's the usual IOBY—In Our Back Yard—contingent advocating for more solar investment at point-of-use, namely solar in the city, not in the desert. There's a long-standing conspiracy theory about the facility poisoning the groundwater with leaked carcinogens from the panels, but studies have shown that has no merit."

Zuri tucked all that away, but there were no giant red flags blaring. "Nothing that indicates this is related to Miller or whatever his project is."

"Not that I can tell," Jeevika agreed.

"The protests just started a few days ago," Lucía said. "*After* the fire on the Island."

Zuri nodded. "After Miller moved the project off-Island, possibly to Palm Springs."

"And at the same time, Renew filed for more expansion."

"By the way," Jeevika added, "someone's leaking to the press that residential backup batteries all over SoCal have been destroyed by the outages. Don't know if it's true, but the media is running with it. Pressure is mounting for an explanation."

"Miller's turning up the heat," Zuri acknowledged. "And, according to Lucía, that damage has been ongoing for some time. I need Miller to think I'm still stewing about this. Put out a release that says USEC is carefully investigating the outages and will have a public statement about this by ten."

"You got it."

"All right, that's enough for me," Zuri said. "Keep me updated, Jeevika. And if you have any inspirational quotes, feel free to send those."

"Will do, Boss!" Her assistant signed off.

"Inspirational quotes?" Lucía asked.

"It makes her happy."

She nodded once like this needed no more explanation. As Zuri and Lucía headed out of her apartment, a message from Jeevika popped up. *"The presence of evil was something to be first recognized, then dealt with, survived, outwitted, triumphed over."* *— Toni Morrison*

It made Zuri smile.

Astra's apartment was in an older residential complex on the far side of the desalination domes and the water tower at the center of the Island. Making good time across the Island's walkways was easier in Lucía's borrowed boots.

"They planned a while ago to move the project

to Palm Springs," Lucía said along the way. "Long enough ago that they had time to lay cable. Just like they ran an extra power line out to the Island."

"My theory is that Ellis 'retired,' but he never stopped working." Zuri glanced around to make sure they weren't overheard, but the Islands were sparsely populated. "Once the world decided not to fund fusion, he moved on to something else. He was only fifty at the time. I remember going to his retirement party and thinking that was awfully young for a brilliant scientist to be quitting the field. But it was a new era. Green-tech was where everything was heading. Fusion was dead. It made sense he would move on... but I didn't expect this."

"Any idea what it is?" Lucía's curiosity had the same intrigue Zuri felt bubbling inside her.

"No. And if he and Miller weren't going to such great pains to cover it up, I'd be less concerned and more curious. The man won a Nobel for his work discovering quasiparticles in plasma before he was forty. That he's involved in this both terrifies and fascinates me."

"I wish I'd known Casimir was really him." Lucía waved open the door to the residential building. "I would have had so many questions. And he seemed really... *nice.*" She gave Zuri a sheepish look.

"I guess that's a stupid thing to say about someone who tried to kill me."

"Oh, no. He absolutely could be charming. Not that I knew him all that well. And I honestly can't see Ellis as the murdering type. That part makes no sense to me." They hushed as they approached Astra's first-floor apartment. Zuri lifted an eyebrow to silently ask if Lucía was ready. She nodded.

Zuri didn't bother knocking. And one perk of being the Greater Los Angeles Area Regional Director of the United States Energy Consortium is you have a lot of access. Including, under certain emergency protocols, private quarters on Power Islands. Zuri waved to bring up the holographic control pad by the door, then pulled up the key in her manager and sent the unlock code.

The apartment was spacious. They quietly stepped through the entranceway and living area, then snuck down the hall. Astra was in her bedroom, clothes tossed all over the bed and floor, hanging on the blinds and covering the upholstered chairs by the sliding glass door.

She was packing things into a brilliant blue suitcase.

"Going somewhere?" Zuri asked as they stepped into the room.

Astra shrieked and spun, half falling back on the bed, wide-eyed and gasping.

Zuri didn't feel the least bit bad about startling the woman half to death.

"Wha... *why are you here?*" She struggled up to standing again, flicking panicked looks between Zuri and Lucía while clutching a pale pink blouse. "You shouldn't be here." She didn't mean *here*, standing in Astra's bedroom, although that had nearly given her a heart attack. She meant *here on the Island*.

"No? Why's that?" Zuri stepped fully into the room with Lucía by her side.

"Shouldn't you... be... working on the outages?" Astra was clearly still reeling from the surprise. "I saw them on the news," she hastily added as she backed away in equal measure.

"The outages you caused?" Lucía's voice was ice cold. Zuri realized at that moment that Lucía hadn't seen Astra since she pulled her out of the sea.

Astra's eyes went a little more round. "I had nothing to do with those!"

"We know it's Miller." Zuri inched closer. Would the woman make a run for it through the sliding glass door? If she did, what would Zuri do? *Tackle her?* Not her favorite idea. "Tell us how he's getting into the AI, Astra. And I promise this won't crash down on your head, at least, not as badly."

"I don't know what you're talking about." She bunched up the blouse in her hand, knuckles white.

"Yes, you do." Lucía was having none of this bullshit. "You told me to leave the Island. To not come back. After I nearly drowned from someone sabotaging my tanks. Now, how did you know to come to the docks at right that moment, Astra? How? If you weren't the one who drained my emergency tank and tampered with my indicators?"

Astra's rapid blinking said Lucía hit right on target.

Zuri stepped closer with Lucía by her side. Together, they were physically crowding Astra until she shrunk against the bed, still holding her pink blouse. "Miller's trying to blame these outages on me," Zuri said. "He wants me to take the fall for all of it. Either way, I may lose my job over this, but Astra... you're going down for attempted murder."

"I didn't do anything!" It was part shriek, part anger. She looked at the crumpled blouse in her hands then at the half-stuffed suitcase.

"You can't run from this," Zuri pressed, afraid the woman would do just that. She dropped her tone, switching from stick to carrot. "Let me help you. I've got powerful connections. I can protect you. Miller made you do this. He's the dangerous one, not you. Tell us how he's getting into the AI, and you don't have to go to jail for him."

She shook her head slowly. "He'll kill me." In that moment, she looked genuinely terrified.

"We won't let him." A tiny bit of sympathy welled up in Zuri, but it dissipated pretty quick. Whatever Miller had threatened her with, she made a *choice*—one that apparently included murder as a viable option. Zuri could see the calculation in Astra's eyes. She would do whatever she thought would serve her best—there was no honor in this woman, just like Miller, even if he was the slimier of the two.

"It's all going to come out, anyway." Lucía gestured to the clothes Astra had been trying to pack. "Where do you think you're going to go? Palm Springs?"

Astra's attention snapped to her.

"Yeah, we know," Zuri said, playing off Lucía's hunch. "We've got the data from the outages. We know you've been working on this for years, just now moving from the Island to the mainland. Did you think all this could stay hidden forever?"

Astra's hands tortured the blouse again. "You

don't understand. You wouldn't believe me, even if I told you."

Lucía was unimpressed. "Try us."

Astra shook her head in short, nervous quirks. "Talk to Ellis. He's there. Palm Springs. Everything you want to know is there. That's all I can say. And you already know that, anyway." She said it with a one-shouldered shrug. Zuri wasn't sure if she was trying to convince them or herself.

Lucía slid her a look that said *At least we know where to go.* Zuri agreed. They weren't going to torture anything more out of Astra. Zuri suspected she didn't even know half of what was going on, specifically the AI manipulation. There was nothing in her file that hinted at her being a coding genius.

Zuri cast a pinched look at the suitcase. "Don't go anywhere." Then she turned to Astra. "I'll let the Coastal Patrol know you're not to leave the Island."

Her face fell slack with surprise but then looked frantic again. "Don't tell Miller I said anything to you!"

Zuri gritted her teeth. "You're not the most pressing thing I have to discuss with Miller." Then she squinted at Astra and swiped up the Island system on her display.

"What are you doing?" Astra asked, her voice hiking up.

"Shutting down your access to the Island's network, including the wider comm systems." Zuri authorized a full lockdown, the emergency protocol for when a power engineer became unstable, a danger to others. She entered her security code then swiped the whole thing away and looked Astra in the eyes. "You're effectively on house arrest. No calls in or out. *Especially to Miller.* Am I clear? And on second thought, I'm having Coastal Patrol come pick you up. Just to keep you from doing something we'll both regret."

Astra just blinked. Like she never expected in a million years for there ever to be *consequences* for this elaborate plot Miller had concocted and she'd willingly gone along with.

Suddenly Zuri was too disgusted to be in the same room any longer. Tipping her head to Lucía, she led the way back out.

The door clicked locked behind her.

Once they were back outside, striding away from Astra's building, Lucía asked, "Are we really going to Palm Springs?"

"Looks like." Zuri cast a look over her shoulder at the sun sinking in the sky. It was going on four in the afternoon. "Miller sucked down the power from the outages, but all we've got is a few traces on a usage map. We need some physical evidence of what they're actually doing at Renew Energy with all that power coming in. And the state regulators have been on me to justify why Renew should be allowed to expand their operation. Plus, the protests give it some urgency. Sounds like an emergency 'fact-finding' inspection by the Regional Director is in order."

Lucía was swiping the air, pulling something up on her display. "It's at least an hour to get back to the harbor—longer if we stick to our private charter. And then it's at least two hours from the harbor to Palm Springs, assuming we can hit each of the light rails just right. Probably double that. Five hours, minimum." She swiped away her display and glanced at Zuri. "We might not make it before Miller's deadline."

"Oh, I think this is the perfect time to use a perk the Regional Director's office possesses but seldom deploys."

Lucía's eyebrows lifted.

"Electrocopter. The IEC has a helipad and a share agreement with the local hospitals, which use them for organ donor matches." She swiped her display to access her USEC official login and put in a request. "The only question is if we can get some fly time before we reach the mainland." But an approval message popped up right away. "Okay. Looks like we're in." She accepted the reservation. "We can fly into Palm Springs International, but I think we need to keep this low-profile after that. Maybe come in as protesters to get through the crowds, then use my credentials to get in. Jeevika's press release should keep Miller wondering what we're up to. Hopefully, Astra won't be able to tip him off. Even rolling up with pre-clearance for an official visit would give him time to hide things. Surprise is our best option, I think."

Lucía grimaced. "Our Island coveralls are probably not the best for going undercover as environmental protesters."

"You're right about that."

It turned out Lucía had left most of her wardrobe on the Island when she fled Astra's murder attempt. The two were close enough in size that Zuri could borrow some work pants and a black t-shirt. While Amani had gone to every manner of protest under the sun, Zuri never had, except when they were little, with their mother. Dressing the part as an adult, even if it was subterfuge, somehow felt right. She and Lucía squeezed together so she could blink a picture of the both of them reflected in her bathroom mirror.

Zuri sent it off to Gwen for approval.

She quickly messaged back. *For the Love of Karl, my cat, you are the most boring protesters ever.*

"Is boring good?" Zuri asked Lucía. She shrugged.

Another message from Gwen. *Did you check the weather? It's hotter than Hell's Kitchen in Palm Springs. Wear shorts. Bring some fucking water and a hat, so you don't die. And if you've got gloves, wear one, left hand only. If there are friendlies in the crowd, they'll see you.*

Who are the friendlies? Zuri messaged back.

There are things the Regional Director doesn't need to know, Z.

Zuri rolled her eyes.

But by the time they left Lucía's apartment, they looked—and Zuri felt—a lot more prepared for a battle neither of them wanted.

EIGHT

Gwen was wrong—Palm Springs was far hotter than Hell's Kitchen.

When Zuri and Lucía climbed out of the electrocopter, it was like stepping into an oven. The sun was lower in the sky, but the waves of heat still shimmering off the tarmac made the small airport surreal. They'd rented a private helipad, so they could lock the electrocopter down to await their return, but Zuri's first instinct was to retreat back inside to the air conditioning. And she wished she'd brought three more water bottles.

They had Gwen on an open audio channel. "You weren't joking about the heat," Zuri said.

"Hyperthermia will fucking kill you." Gwen's voice had no humor whatsoever. "It's dry, or you'd be dying already. The human body is not meant to exist in environments above its internal 98.6 deg F. Above that, your sweat keeps you from cooking from the inside out, but if the humidity's too high, then sweating is useless. Then you're fucked."

"I'm definitely sweating," Zuri reported in.

"Start drinking that water you brought now," Gwen continued. "And don't stop. Refill whenever you have a chance. The protests will have water and shade stations, guaranteed, maybe showers because this has been going on a while. That's your oasis. But you gotta get there first."

Lucía was already sipping at her water bottle as they marched across the brutal pavement. Zuri could feel the heat through the soles of her boots. She opened an audio channel to her assistant as well— they needed all the support they could get for this operation.

"Jeevika, I'm having second thoughts about walking from the airport to Renew's office complex. It's over two miles in this heat." The protests were apparently clustered at the main entrance to Renew Energy. The solar panels themselves were spread all over Palm Springs, taking over the parched golf courses now rendered useless as tourist destinations, given the climate-driven heat and water scarcity.

Zuri had seen the solar farms from the air, a patch-work of black, rectangular lakes that sparkled in the sun. All their kilowatts fed into the main plant area, which had an office tower in addition to massive transformers for stepping up the power and an underground battery storage area kept away from the heat.

"I thought you might want an autocar." Jeevika had that cheerful tone that said she'd already thought three steps ahead of Zuri and was just glad Zuri had finally arrived at the party. "Weather Service says it's 110 degrees F. That's borderline danger tempera-ture. I've been trying to hail an autocar service, but unfortunately, there's nothing I can find in Palm Springs beyond their light rail, which is really just a line out of the area."

Zuri brushed away the sweat gathering on her brow and squinted at the structures bordering the helipad area. She could see why the autocar service she took for granted was nowhere to be found in Palm Springs. The titular palm trees still lined the streets, but everything else was dead—no grass or even desert landscaping, just baked dirt and an occa-sional tumbleweed trapped against a dust-brown brick wall. The low-lying architecture was Fossilized Last-Century, the way towns once-prosperous looked after the climate-driven heat baked the business and population out of them. She'd seen more than one climate shantytown, and that's what Palm Springs apparently was now. Makeshift awnings stretched between the buildings and even across the streets, providing a walk-path shaded from the incessant sun.

It was slightly ironic to have a solar farm here. The intense heat actually *reduced* the effectiveness of the solar panels—the state had several more-efficient solar farms in the fields where Southern California's abundant crops were grown, namely farther north where there was less heat and more water. The agrophotovoltaic symbiosis worked well—crops were shaded and used less water, the panels harvested sun but in lower-heat conditions. Palm Springs *wasn't* the perfect location for a solar farm. Its main advantage was consisting of previously disturbed land—no environmental issues and cheap to acquire—in a place where it was now unrelentingly terrible for human occupation.

The only problem was the stubborn humans who still lived there.

"Let's go through the helipad terminal and get more water," Lucía suggested, and she got no argument from Zuri.

"One to two quarts per hour," Gwen said in an approving tone. "And that's just to stay even."

Zuri was so drenched with sweat by the time they reached the terminal that going through the revolving door to the precious air conditioning inside felt like stepping into a freezer. Her whole-body shiver made it hard to refill her water bottle from the station. Lucía bought two more from the kiosk and tucked them in her shorts' cargo pockets. Zuri's had none, probably because her shorts were actually pajamas. She was regretting that choice, even though they were lighter weight. Lucía would just have to be their water carrier.

Zuri braced herself for stepping outside again. It was even more brutal the second time.

"I'm starting to understand why the citizens of Palm Springs are pissed about anything that brings even a half a degree of extra heat to their city." Zuri knew the politics of situating renewables was sticky —they brought jobs and electricity but took away landscapes, views, and land. People had to live *some-where*—but they also needed electricity to survive. While most of the power from Renew's solar farms was exported to the metro area, Palm Springs did benefit from them as well—the desalination domes at the nearby Salton Sea couldn't run without all that juice, not to mention the Sea would have long-ago run out of water if it weren't pumped from the ground or from the Sea of Cortez to the south. All of that took energy.

Living took energy. It was a tough balance, one she was very familiar with.

"My tracker says you're outside again," Gwen said.

"You're tracking my chip?"

"Yes?" Gwen said this like she thought the heat had started to cook Zuri's brain. "Okay, you're on the airport perimeter drive, heading North. Keep going until you hit Vista Solar and go east. That will take you right into Renew Energy's main complex. Past that, hugging the mountains is where the transmission cables are. You probably can't see them from where you are, but they dump into the plant."

They hiked in sweaty silence for a while.

The temperature got legitimately hotter as they turned down Vista Solar Drive as if the dial on the oven was cranked just a little more. The solar panels along the road angled toward the sun, a mechanical phototropism run by bots and the very electricity they gathered. The black panels were endless, climbing right up the side of the mountains that hemmed the valley. Up ahead, a mirrored tower rose taller than anything around it. The shimmering heat created a mirage of water as if the Renew Energy building were a magical castle floating in the desert.

"We're getting close," Lucía said for the benefit of Gwen and Jeevika, listening in on their panting through the heat.

"Any luck on blocking Miller's hack?" Zuri asked.

"Not yet." Gwen sounded more than a little irate about that. "I keep thinking we're close, but then something doesn't track, and we're back to square one. Basically, we're trying to simulate what he did, offline so it doesn't wreck people's power, and we're not getting the same result. But I think we're closer."

Zuri drank the last of her water bottle while Gwen talked, then capped it. "Let me know. We need that, regardless, but if we had it now, this would be a lot less fraught."

"Understood." Gwen hesitated. "But this might be your only chance to find out if they've got secret labs going inside Renew Energy. Element of surprise. Private company shenanigans. All that."

"Right." Zuri handed her empty bottle to Lucía, who swapped it for a full one.

"Once you get inside, you're looking for Jarrod Ungar," Jeevika reminded her. "He's the facility manager and the one who filed the petition to the commissioners to expand the facility."

"Tell him you know about the secret cable," Gwen added. "That should throw him."

"Got it." They were getting close. "I'm leaving the line open, but let's keep the chatter to a minimum." She peered at Lucía, who seemed to be holding up okay under the heat. "You ready?"

"To muscle our way through protesters into a private utility company where we're definitely not wanted?" Lucía asked. "Or to potentially find out what the hell was worth trying to kill me over?"

Zuri shook her head. "Yes."

"Ready." Lucía smirked, then took a chug of her water bottle. She actually looked prepped, even eager, for this. Zuri didn't feel nearly as confident as Lucía looked, but she was 1000% more ready than she'd been a few hours ago. Marching through the heat to take on a corporate plot to steal power from the people? *This was something Amani would do.* Using her position and authority to demand answers from people who should be held accountable so the system would work for everyone? *That was something Zuri would do.*

She wasn't her twin. She couldn't fill the Amani-sized hole in the world, much less in her heart and in her life. But she could honor her sister by being the best of what both tried to be in the world. *Doing your part when the time came.* That's what their mama always said they were obliged to. No single person could rescue the world from all its sins and bad judgment, not to mention all its past petroleum usage. But everyone could do their part. You didn't always know what it was until it happened. And you would miss it if you weren't paying attention. If you didn't keep an open heart and an open mind. Often it was exactly the worst thing at the worst possible time. Life was *not* convenient. Even with all the blessings Zuri had in her life, she knew that much. When the time came, it was usually the last thing you were planning that day... and yet doing your part almost always ended up the best thing you did that day. Or that year.

Zuri carried that sure knowledge with her as she marched into the crowd with Lucía by her side. Everyone was hot and tired and slippery with sweat. Gwen was right—there were water stations and shade areas. The people standing out in the sun rotated into the shade while others took their place. They stood with their signs—*No More Heat* and *Build It Where You Burn It*—at the gated entrance to the facility, which was guarded by a shack that seemed to normally be staffed by one security guard, but which now had half a dozen, two at a time rotating into the air conditioning inside. A half-hearted chant rose up and then subsided. Zuri couldn't tell what it was. The protesters wore regular clothes, no coordinated shirts or bandanas, everyone simply dressing to survive the heat. She noticed a couple with gloves, left hand only like Gwen had instructed. *Friendlies.* Still not sure what that meant, but she caught the eye of one—a young white man—who watched her as she made her way up to the guard shack. The protesters kept back, maintaining a ten-foot gap between themselves and the guards.

Zuri strode right into that demilitarized zone.

Lucía trailed a step behind her. The guard out in front, standing in the road leading into the facility, scowled as she approached. He was big—over six feet and muscular under his lightweight uniform—and he looked as miserable in the heat as everyone else.

"Move back!" he barked when she'd crossed half the gap.

It made her jump and stop. Then she took another deliberate step forward, close enough to speak without shouting. "I'm the Regional Director of USEC—"

"And I'm the Secretary of Defense," he snapped. "I said *move back.*"

"Voiceprint me."

He gave a look of disgust. "I'm not voice printing shit. Now step back, or I'm going to have to—"

"My name is Zuri Hill-Gray." She raised her voice—the officers in the shack, the protesters, everyone could hear her now. "I am the Los Angeles Regional Director of the United States Energy Consortium, and I am here on a fact-finding inspection of the Renew Energy facility."

The guards in the shack had come to attention. The protesters behind her had stopped their rumblings. The guard in front of her was flicking looks between her and the shack like he was waiting for some signal about what to do.

She lowered her voice again, stepping closer and peering at his nameplate. "Mr. Erlich, I strongly recommend you voice print me. Unless you want Renew to lose their license to operate this facility. I'd imagine your job would be cut first."

He blinked, hesitated. "We didn't have any notice about—"

"Surprise inspection, Erlich," Lucía said. "Catch up."

Zuri suppressed the manic urge to laugh, especially when Erlich's eyes flashed and seemed to reconsider his hesitation. Gwen was chortling in her ear.

A guard from the shack shouted, "Checks out!"

Erlich gritted his teeth and swiped up something on his display. "Voiceprint." It was a request, although a begrudging one.

Zuri repeated her name and title. After a moment, the electronic gate behind him clicked unlocked. Erlich grudgingly stepped aside as Zuri and Lucía passed. She didn't pay his glare any mind.

The air conditioning inside Renew Energy's lobby was a blessed relief.

There was no one to greet them, so after a moment of reveling in the cool air, Lucía said, "Let's go." The lobby was two stories tall, with offices overhead, but Zuri's instinct said they should go *below*. Lucía's must have been the same because they wordlessly headed to the bank of elevators, and she waved at the button to go down. As they waited for the elevator, Lucía said, "Stairs might be faster."

Zuri nodded, and they scouted down the hallway, looking for the stairwell. A woman hurried out one of the windowless doors, nearly ran into Lucía, then scuttled down the hallway in her white lab coat. But not before Zuri caught a glimpse of her badge.

Zuri had been inside many public utility facilities. Most employees didn't have badges at all—if you passed security to get in, that was clearance enough. The few that had badges were for secure hard-coded access to things like nuclear materials or sensitive technology areas that might compromise operations, like the control center for an entire hydro-electric dam. They were clearly identified with picture IDs and encoded biometric data, and most importantly, the security-granting authority. Usually in sharp-contrasting symbology that was further security patterned to prevent counterfeiting.

This was not a Renew Energy badge.

She had only a glimpse, but what she saw ran a chill through her that had nothing to do with the sweat still clinging to her body. *DARPA*. In bold blue letters stamped over a gridded globe. The Defense Advanced Research Projects Agency had a legitimate interest in energy technologies all over the United States. Zuri had even attended one of DARPA's energy development conferences early in her career. And she could think of zero reasons a DARPA researcher would be found scurrying through a hallway at Renew Energy solar plant.

Zero *good* reasons... and a whole lot of bad ones.

Lucía was looking at her strangely. "You okay?"

"Did you see that—"

"*There* you are, Madam Director!"

Zuri jumped.

A man hurried toward them from the elevators, his hard shoes echoing down the hall. He stopped short and bowed deeply. "I had no idea you'd be visiting us, Ms. Hill-Gray!" he gushed, a million-watt smile covering even more nervousness.

"The Director would like to speak with the plant manager," Lucía tried.

"That's me!" The man literally clapped his hands together. "Jarrod Ungar, at your service." Then his false-cheerfulness looked even more pained. "You both look like you've been through the inferno, as we call it. Please, let me get you some water, and let's get you comfortable. We have a lounge with all kinds of refreshments—"

Zuri held up her hand. "That won't be necessary."

Jarrod looked like she'd smashed his favorite toy.

"Jarrod, let me tell you why I'm here."

"Yes. Please." Jarrod's hands were tormenting each other, but his smile didn't falter.

"You've got an extra power line coming into this facility from the Inland grid," Zuri started. "An unauthorized power line."

"I'm sorry?" Jarrod blinked like he couldn't possibly have heard her correctly.

"I'd like to know how and when that power line was strung, and by whose authorization."

"I, um..." He was frowning now, one of his hands working free to hold up a finger. "Let me make sure I understand what you're saying, Madam Director." Then he grimaced like he couldn't quite figure out how to tell the Regional Director of USEC she was barking mad.

The elevator dinged behind him, which distracted Jarrod even further.

But it was Zuri's turn to be shocked.

Jim Ellis strolled toward the three of them with a tight smile on his face.

"It's all right, Jarrod." He clapped a hand on the man's shoulder, and the relief nearly melted Jarrod's face. "The Director and I go way back, don't we, Zuri?"

"I suppose we do." Zuri's eyes had gone wide.

"And you brought Ms. Ramirez with you! Excellent." To Jarrod, he said, "I'll take it from here," effectively dismissing the man. He bowed and quickly retreated. Ellis turned back to Zuri. "Let's talk in private, shall we?"

"Ellis, what's going on here?" Zuri asked, point-blank. She wasn't so sure going *anywhere* with the man was a good idea. Lucía's skeptical look seemed to confirm that. *"Don't do it, Z,"* a voice literally whispered in her ear, making Zuri jolt. She'd forgotten Gwen and Jeevika were still on the line, listening in.

Ellis sighed and stepped over to the elevator, summoning it with a wave. "How about I show you instead?" A small smile played on his face, but he was serious about the two of them getting in that elevator. Especially when it quickly dinged open. When they hesitated, he gave them an exasperated look. "Well, I can't talk about it in the lobby, now, can I?"

Zuri grimaced and looked to Lucía. "You can stay if you like."

"Hell, no. *Ma'am.*"

That made her smile. She stepped into the elevator with Ellis despite the whispered *Dammit* coming from Gwen in her ear. Lucía joined her, and Ellis pulled a manual keycard from his pocket and swiped it near the holopad.

The elevator closed and dropped.

"I wish you hadn't gotten involved, Zuri," Ellis said, with what sounded like real regret in his voice. "And *you.*" He wagged a finger at Lucía. "You're even more stubborn than I thought." But there was strangely no menace in his voice as if he were their father gently scolding them for mixing it up with the wrong kind of people after he warned them not to.

Only Zuri was sure *Ellis* was the wrong kind of people, at this point.

The elevator lurched to a stop and opened. The three stepped out into one of the largest underground, temperature-controlled industrial battery storage bunkers Zuri had ever seen. It stretched farther than she could actually see, only the lights nearest them lit up, while the large, humming black boxes the size of autocars stretched out, lined up into the distance. How far? Zuri could only guess, but Ellis's hard-soled shoes echoed as though the underground storage was vast.

"You're showing me batteries?" Zuri asked. There were a *lot*... but that wasn't anything worth keeping secret.

"No, of course not." He gave her a look like she was being stupid. "But this area is secure, so we won't have any hapless plant managers stumbling upon us. I argued for bringing you into this, Zuri. Why try to go around the Regional Director when you could have her co-operation? It made no sense to me, but you see..." He shrugged. "I'm only the scientist. I'm not in charge. You know how that goes."

"Why would you have done either?" Lucía asked. "If you wanted to keep doing fusion research, why couldn't you just... go somewhere else? There must have been someone in the world who would have funded your work."

"At the time? No." That small smile was back. "But now... now funding is no longer a problem." He tapped his temple. "I told Miller to watch you, Ms. Ramirez. Not to underestimate your intelligence."

Lucía crossed her arms and glared. "You mean, you told him to kill me."

"What?" He looked genuinely shocked. "*No.* I said nothing of the kind."

Zuri watched as the realization stole over this brilliant man's face that *he* had underestimated something rather dramatically. Namely, Miller.

"He threatened you. Miller." It was a question from Ellis, directed at Lucía.

"A few times, actually. But I think it was Astra who tried to drown me."

Ellis's wariness fell into a scowl. "That is unfortunate."

Lucía looked unimpressed. "Yes. That was my

exact thought when I was out of air a hundred feet underwater."

He pursed his lips as if Lucía were an uncooperative child to not instantly forgive attempted murder.

"Ellis, you're not doing fusion here," Zuri said, dropping her voice to the most serious level she had. "Or back on the Island. At least, no kind of fusion research I'm familiar with, not at any scale. You're stealing energy but not *enough*—and unless you have a secret fleet of lab assistants helping you, not just Astra, I'm not sure what you've been up to. But it's either illegal or immoral... or else you wouldn't be doing all of *this*." She gestured in the air to indicate all the insane lengths he and Miller had gone to in order to keep the project secret.

His eyes flashed. "I am doing something that will change the world."

"Is that why DARPA's involved?" She grimaced. "Dammit, Ellis. What have you done?"

He glowered at her. "The world declared my work *ridiculous*. They declared fusion dead. As if we weren't on the edge of monumental breakthroughs every week!"

"What, so now you want revenge?" Lucía demanded. "Is that why you think you're entitled to drain power from ordinary people all over the city?"

He waved her off. "That is unimportant."

"Not to them," Lucía ground out. "Or the rest of us."

Zuri held up a hand to stop her. To Ellis, she said, "You brought us down here for a reason. What is it?"

Ellis laced his hands and touched his index fingers to his lips like he was weighing whether to tell her his big secret or not. "I want to bring you in on this, Zuri," he said finally. "I truly do. As I said, I thought that was prudent from the start. You were a talented engineer. You had a keen sense of the science. You'd be an asset to the project. But once you're in..." He flicked a look to Lucía and seemed to include her. "There's no getting out. You can't know this and ever go back."

"I'll be the judge of that." Zuri was ready to clobber him with her still-full water bottle. Or unleash Lucía on him—she was simmering mad.

"It doesn't work that way, Zuri." He frowned at her. "You should know better than that. And I told you: I'm not in charge here. I'm only the scientist." He was still hinting around, and it was driving her mad.

"The scientist who invented something so world-changing that it has to be kept a secret from every-one." She stuffed it full of sarcasm.

But Ellis only seemed delighted. "Yes."

Zuri sighed. "Goddammit, Ellis, I'm not going to play charades with you—"

"I *am* sorry, Zuri."

"Just tell me, then."

His attention flicked to the side, something in his display. "I promise, I will try to fight to bring you on."

"*What?*" Dread rushed into her stomach.

A half-second later, the elevator opened.

And Miller strode out.

NINE

Ellis had been stalling. Of course.

Zuri cursed under her breath.

"Is that any kind of greeting?" Miller asked, smile wide. "I see Ellis has kept you entertained with our vast battery collection."

She had words for Miller, but none were helpful.

"Is that *Miller?*" Gwen hissed in her ear.

"Should I call for the police?" Jeevika's voice was strung tight.

"Miller. I should have known," Zuri said to get them to shut up.

He sneered. "I should have known you would never do the sensible thing, Zuri."

She narrowed her eyes. "Trust me. You do *not* know me."

Miller shrugged. "Perhaps." He slid a look to Ellis. "Which is why I was correct in not bringing her on board." He faced her again. "I don't *trust* people, Zuri, unlike your hapless management style that's allowed all of this to exist under your nose for..." He facetiously checked his display. "About ten years now."

She bit back the smart-ass retort that jumped into her mouth. Because Miller was giving her information. That meant either he would kill her, or he was slipping up in his arrogance. She had two witnesses on the line, but she was cursing herself for not initiating a recording of this. Any motion to do so now and Miller would notice. "Ten years. That's when we towed Power Island One back into US waters. That's when you laid the secret power cable. And when you started planning the project." They'd figured this out on their own, but now Miller was confirming it.

"Plans were well underway by then." Miller smirked. "With people like Ellis, who understood the stakes. And people whose greed or emotional needs were well understood—enough to keep them under control. I didn't know how much trouble you would become, Zuri, or I would have found a way to sabotage your career sooner."

"Right. Fuck you for that, by the way."

"Tsk tsk. Language, Zuri." He flicked a look at Lucía. "Not in front of the children." He was having a good laugh with this. Lucía clenched a full water bottle in her hand and looked ready to club him.

Zuri kept her voice steady. "What I don't understand, Miller, is what makes you think you can orchestrate all this and not have it come out, eventually."

"And yet I've done precisely that for years." The gloat was fully formed on his face. "Power isn't measured in kilowatts, Zuri. It's measured by who and what you can *stop,* as well as what you can do, right under people's noses. People will believe what you tell them to believe, especially if you say it often and with conviction. It's especially easy if it makes their lives just a little more comfortable. A little easier. Or even better, if it makes their lives *worse*—if there's some sacrifice they have to make, but it's all for the greater good, you see. No need to question it. No need to think too hard about anything. They accept it and even feel good about it. Weave those outages into their everyday lives, tap a little power they'll never notice missing, and that's just their reality."

"Oh, we *noticed*, Miller." Lucía's glare would set the man on fire if it had any more heat.

There was something off about that little rant, but it was hard to tell what—Miller simply disgusted Zuri at an atomic level. "You don't *own* Power Island One. That literally belongs to the world. Especially the fusion labs. That research was funded by every nation on earth. Whatever you were doing down there, *even after* the labs were shut down, it's public domain." And then it clicked. She swung her pinched look at Ellis. "*That's* why you kept it secret. It was something you'd *already* discovered. Something the world could lay claim to under the IEC agreements. But you were pissed they shut you down. You wanted it for yourself."

"If there had been a brain among them—"

"*Ellis.*" Miller's rage was instant-on, full-strength. It shut Ellis down but only confirmed what Zuri had sussed out. Miller and Ellis weren't out to change the world—they were out to get rich. By changing the world. Or destroying it. DARPA wasn't hanging out in the hallways of the solar farm for kicks.

Zuri had never seen Miller so angry. His pale cheeks were actually turning red.

"I have been more than fair with you," he hissed

at her. "This is your last chance. Make the announcement now. Take responsibility for the outages. I don't care what excuse you make for USEC's incompetence in this regard, just make it believable. And then resign. Or hold onto your job, if you can. I don't care. But walk away from this. Now. Or I will crush you under an absolutely catastrophic collapse of the grid you've so myopically devoted your life to."

"Let me think about that..." She tapped her chin in a faux position of contemplation. Then she stared him dead in the eyes. "Gonna have to say no to that."

Miller let out a long, low breath. The red was fading from his cheeks. "Then you're free to go."

She lifted her eyebrow and dashed a look to Lucía. She was strung tight but not moving.

Miller swept his hand to the elevators. "You might want to get back to LA before the blackout tsunami hits. And remember, Zuri: you chose this."

Zuri gave him a look like he was a monster, then strode quickly to the elevator. It opened as soon as she waved. Lucía hurried to join her inside. Miller turned to stare at them as the doors closed.

"*Holy shit,* Zuri." Lucía let out a breath like she'd been holding it the whole time.

"I agree," Gwen said in her ear. "Zuri gets the *Oh No You Didn't* Award for today. Well done."

"I have the Palm Springs police on standby." Jeevika's voice was hushed. Zuri knew her assistant well enough to know she was thoroughly freaked.

"Jeevika, we're fine. Call off the cavalry."

She could hear her exhale. "Yes, ma'am."

The elevator opened. Zuri hesitated when they stepped out, glancing back down the hall to the door where the DARPA employee had emerged.

"I don't think we should push our luck," Lucía said, eyes wide.

"No, you're right." Zuri pursed her lips. Somehow, she would get back in here to figure out what the hell Miller and Ellis were up to. Not personally, though. Next time, she doubted Miller would let her walk away. "We need to get back to LA. Gwen, you heard Miller, right? He's about to blow up the AI."

"I heard. We've got several new patches in for safeguards, but those will mostly mitigate the harm after it happens. We're still trying to devise a block. I'm sorry, Z. I thought we could sort this in time."

"Well, that's my fault." Zuri pushed through the revolving door to the outside. "I pushed up your timeline with our little side quest."

"All right, I'm hanging up," Gwen said. "We'll do everything we can to hold off the storm until you get back."

"Jeevika, you can go too," Zuri said as they reached the guard gate. "I'll check in with you when we're on the way."

"I would like to stay on the line, Madam Director."

Zuri could hear the stress in her voice. "That's fine, too."

The guards at the gate buzzed them through. The protesters were still there. The heat seemed to have waned a degree or two, and it was enough to inject some new life into the crowd. They were chanting again, holding up their signs. A few looked their way as Zuri and Lucía worked through the crowd.

"I was thinking we could dig back through Ellis's old papers," Lucía said. "The public-facing ones at least. All that research at Energy Island..."

Zuri edged through the crowd, raising her voice to be heard over the chanting. "Good thinking. All of that has to be public—" Someone slammed into her. "Sorry," she said reflexively, but then someone else grabbed her arm. "Hey!" They were dragging her forward, the same direction she had been going. She struggled against the man's hold, but his grip was too strong. He was one of the protesters, his hat pulled low and a water-drenched handkerchief covering his face. They'd reached the edge of the crowd, but he kept going.

"Jeevika!" she gasped. "Call the police!"

There was only static on the line. *A blocker. Shit.* She pushed and yelled. Her struggle went unnoticed in the chanting. As he dragged her from the crowd, she saw another man had grabbed Lucía. He'd lifted her bodily off the ground, his arms wrapped around her, pinning her arms to her sides. She was yelling and kicking, but Zuri could barely hear her, and she was only a half dozen feet away. The whole thing took only seconds. A couple of the protesters noticed, frowning in their direction. The man grabbing her yanked her attention away. They'd reached an autocar parked on the side of the road. The doors sprung open.

Like hell, she was going in there. *"Help!"* Zuri yelled, flailing and trying to twist away.

The man who had Lucía dumped her on the ground. Then he pointed something at her—and she convulsed.

"Stop it!" Zuri's throat hurt from the scream.

"Shut up!" the man hissed in her ear. He shoved something hard into her side. "Or you'll get the same."

Her heart seized, her throat closed up. *She froze.*

Fear reaction, she told her brain. *Breathe.* She watched the other man lift Lucía's still-shaking body into the car. It was a four-seater, two seats front-facing, two to the rear. Lucía lay twitching on the floor in the center. The man who grabbed her climbed in, stepping over her. The twitches had to mean Lucía was alive.

"Get in." Her kidnapper barely loosened his grip, just enough to allow her to climb in the autocar herself. He came in right after her, slapping the button to close the doors.

Oh, God. She'd gotten them both killed. These men were going to kill them.

She turned to him as the doors closed. "You don't have to do this."

He ignored her, swiping up something in his display. He was laying in the destination for the autocar. Somewhere they could be murdered. *What could she do?* Override the command? Did her chip even work? Her hand shook as she tried to swipe open a search. Everything was blocked. The man just smirked at her.

The car lurched forward... *and stopped.*

The two men whipped their attention to the forward end of the car. A protester stood directly in front of it, hands out. One had a glove. The car's autodetect had stopped it. Another man joined him, standing a foot away from the car, blocking the car's ability to move. Her kidnapper was swiping furiously, but he couldn't override the protocols to make an autocar drive into a crowd.

And a crowd was quickly gathering around them.

Someone tried the doors, but they were locked. Zuri lunged to open them, but the manual latch was disabled. One protester pounded on the window. Several others beat on the front and back, shouting and making demands. The two kidnappers were freaked. One started cursing, and the other told him to shut the fuck up.

"Let us go," Zuri said, hastily. "That's all they want." *Friendlies.* Zuri was going to kiss Gwen when she got back to the office.

The kidnapper next to her was swiping up a call. "Do you fucking see this?" Whoever was on the other end was saying things that did not make him happy.

Then the car started to rock.

"Fuck!" The man slammed his hand against the window to keep from falling over.

The protesters were pushing the car, a dozen on each side... *trying to tip it.* Zuri eased to the floor, grabbing hold of Lucía's shirt to keep her from sliding. She was moaning, and her eyes were open, but she didn't seem able to move her limbs.

The rocking escalated. The protesters were getting more tilt with each pass.

"You have to let us out." Zuri braced, hands and feet, trying to keep both her and Lucía from banging around. "You let us out, and I'll tell them to let you go." She had no idea if she'd keep that promise. Or if the mob would listen.

The man was still on the call. But it must have ended because he said, "Fuck!" and lunged for her.

"No, no, no!" she screeched, trying to fend him off. But his hand was around her throat, pinning her against the back seat before she could do anything to stop him.

His face loomed over hers. "You keep your mouth shut." His hot breath coated her face. "Or we'll come for you." A tremendous pounding started on the car. His hand on her throat was cutting off her air. Just as black stars swam in front of her eyes, he released her.

Someone was pounding on the window with the pole of a protest sign.

"What the fuck are we doing?" the second kidnapper demanded.

The first didn't answer, just swiped something on his display.

The doors clicked unlocked. Zuri lunged for the button, banging it. The doors slid open. A round of shouts went up, and the rocking ceased.

"Help her," Zuri cried, cradling Lucía's head. Three protesters reached into the car, each grabbing hold somewhere on Lucía's legs and dragging her out. Zuri came along, and more hands helped lift her out of the autocar. As soon as she was clear, the doors started to close. Protesters shoved their way in the gap, keeping it from closing. An electric sound buzzed, and those blocking the doors suddenly convulsed and fell back. Other protesters caught them before they hit the ground, but the doors closed and locked before more could stop them.

Zuri crouched on the ground with Lucía, cradling her head to keep it off the red-hot pavement and making sure she didn't get trampled. But the "mob" wasn't unruly. They had kind of stepped back, uncertain now that Zuri and Lucía were free. Someone brought blankets for Lucía and the others who'd been zapped. They helped Zuri get one under Lucía, so the ground wouldn't burn her.

The Renew Energy guards stood by their shack, watching. Doing nothing.

Unbelievable. But Zuri had no energy for that right now.

To the protesters still surrounding the autocar, she called out, "Just let them go!" She didn't want anyone else to get hurt.

They hesitated. But the heat was still a nightmare, and most were already exhausted by it. One by one, they peeled off. When the last one cleared the way, the autocar took off, speeding away.

Zuri sighed in relief.

One of the protesters—the first man who'd stopped the autocar, the one with the glove—knelt next to her and Lucía. "You okay?"

She nodded.

"I'll get the medic." He raised his fist and made a circling motion.

"Thank you." Zuri didn't want to cry, but the shock wrenched tears out of her. They leaked down her face.

"Your friend's going to be okay. It's probably just a slap-tap." At her confused look, he added, "A shock weapon used to control people." He squinted. "It's a military weapon. Not usually used in places like this."

The medic arrived a moment later, a slender woman with pink hair, and she immediately started checking over Lucía. She was moaning less, eyes now squeezed shut, but she was trying to roll over on her side, which the medic seemed to think was a good idea because she helped.

Suddenly, Zuri's display flashed up a dozen calls and messages. *The blocker.* With the kidnappers gone, her chip had rebooted. An emergency-coded audio call blared for attention. It was Jeevika.

Zuri answered it. "Jeevika—"

"Oh, my, God, Zuri! Are you okay?"

"Yes."

"What happened? You cut out, there was nothing but static, and I couldn't reach you!"

"I'm fine." She was breathless, and her throat hurt. Her fingers felt along her neck and found sore spots. "I need an ambulance for Lucía, though."

"What?"

"Jeevika," she said as calmly as she could. "I'm all right. But Lucía was attacked with a shock weapon, and I need some medical personnel here right away to check on her. Does Palm Springs have a hospital?"

"Yes." Her assistant had summoned some kind of calming spell because her voice was back to the *extremely-stressed-but-working-the-problem* tone she'd had through most of this. *"The police are*

already on the way. I'll tell them you need medical assistance as well."

"Thank you. I'll catch you up as soon as I can."

"I'm just... going to leave the line open, okay?" The tremble was back.

"Yes. That's okay."

Someone handed Zuri some water. She drank the entire thing down, and it almost made her sick. But she settled on a corner of the blanket next to Lucía's legs. She was moving a little, stretching, but not getting up in a hurry or anything. Which was just as well.

Zuri just stared at the pavement for a few minutes.

Those men had tried to kill her. Tried to kill both of them. It wasn't hard to guess who sent them. Or what the threat to keep her mouth shut meant.

She couldn't even feel fear about that right now. Just amazement that she'd survived to sit on red-hot pavement and think about it.

Another call buzzed her out of her fugue. It was Gwen.

"Hey, Z! I've got some good news."

"I could use some of that."

"You sound kind of raspy. You okay?"

"Yeah." Zuri just left it at that for the moment.

She wouldn't be coming back to LA, no matter how much things were melting down, not until she knew Lucía was all right. "What do you have for me?"

"We found a block that works." The pride in Gwen's voice was unmistakable. "I was right. He was encoding a signal in the interface between the AI systems. It was like a cascade triggered by a specific set of variances in the Inland grid. Still not sure how he created that, but we found the receptor for it on the metro grid side. We put a blocker in that, replayed a sim from this afternoon, and that effectively prevented the outages. So, we're about 99% sure that'll stop Miller whenever he decides to launch his tsunami. Any idea how long he'll wait to pull the trigger?"

Zuri felt gingerly along the side of her neck. "I think he just did."

"Really? Excellent. Because we're all green lights here. 100%."

"That is good news."

And then she had to hang up because the police had arrived. She would explain to Gwen later. And Jeevika. And she'd get Lucía whatever she needed to make sure she was okay.

Then she had an important choice to make.

TEN

Zuri admired her twist out in the mirror.

"Lookin' pretty good." Her reflection nodded in agreement. She'd trimmed off her frizzy ends, and Auntie Vivian had shown her how to do a two-strand twist out, using lots of her magic Twist-and-Shout cream to give the twists better definition. It had taken a few tries—she'd switched to a side-part and separated the twists for more volume—but her new look was coming together. It wasn't Amani's big, perfect afro. It wasn't the natural short-crop Zuri had worn most of her professional life. This was stylish and new, with lots of bounce and swing.

More free. "See?" she said to the mirror. "I can do new things."

She didn't need to see Amani in the mirror to know she would have approved.

That choice was easy.

"Hey, babe." Denzel poked his head into their bedroom. "I'm taking the kids down to the park. They want to give Ruby her crown."

"I'll be there in a minute."

Her husband gave her a smile that filled her heart. It said *I see you. And I know you'll keep that promise.*

Such change a week could make.

Jayden and Audre had spent the morning gathering wildflowers from the Hillstead, and Denzel had the patience of a saint teaching them how to weave a crown for their cousin for her big performance. Each month someone on the Hillstead shared some kind of thing—art or music or a reading. Her father had started it, so of course, they'd kept on after he was gone. Everyone took turns, and this was little Ruby's debut. She'd been so quiet since her mama's death. Everyone was beside themselves when her seven-year-old self volunteered.

Zuri was glad she could bring her whole self to this.

As her husband slipped away and shouted for

the kids, a message popped up on Zuri's display. It was from Jeevika.

"*All paradises, all utopias are designed by who is not there, by the people who are not allowed in.*" – *Toni Morrison*

Zuri smiled and swiped up a keyboard to message back. *It's Saturday. I'm off the clock.*

And a well-deserved break, too! Just wanted to let you know your appointment with Commissioner Sato is all set for Monday.

Zuri thanked her and signed off.

It was risky, but she'd made her choice.

The world was no utopia—if she hadn't known that before, this last week would have convinced her. Miller tried to murder her and Lucía in Palm Springs, just to stop them from uncovering whatever secret energy technology he and Ellis had discovered. She could go public with that, trigger all manner of investigations, but that almost certainly wouldn't stop him. He would scurry deeper underground like the mole he was. The thugs he'd sent to kill them had already disappeared. She had almost no real evidence tying Miller directly to anything.

And besides, he'd quit USEC and taken Astra with him. Someone had busted into her apartment on the Island and liberated her from the lockdown.

The next day, both tendered their resignations. Just yesterday, she'd heard through the USEC chat stream they were now working for Renew Energy. An innocent job change in anyone's eyes—the kind that happened all the time in an industry filled with players—except this wasn't. Zuri knew Miller was carrying on with his plans, the ones he'd been enacting for ten years under everyone's noses.

Including hers.

She didn't feel bad about that, knowing the lengths to which Miller had gone. And she didn't feel bad about her decision to work this from the inside. First, she couldn't risk everyone's lives—hers, Lucía's, both of their families. Miller was a murderous, scheming coward, and if he thought she was still hunting him, he wouldn't hesitate to escalate. But second, she didn't think public exposure and sending investigators after Miller would actually work. You can't conduct secret experiments on a secret energy technology, hidden away on a historic Energy Island, without having protectors in powerful places. Miller didn't do this alone. It would take working this from the inside—Miller believing she'd taken his threats and retreated—to have any chance of uncovering what was truly going on.

So, Zuri took the hit on her career. She told most

of the truth. That USEC had been hacked, suffering an attack by unknown parties who'd discovered a weakness in their AI system. She'd announced to the world that she didn't know who had done it but that they'd secured the grid against future attacks. All true... except for the not-knowing part.

She regretted the tarnish that USEC took with that announcement. Worse was the hit on the trust USEC had built for decades. They guaranteed people publicly-funded, reliable power if they would agree to the solar installs and battery backups, the demand-side management and the occasional outage. USEC promised the outages were necessary and rigorously controlled, so they could all make maximum usage of their renewable energy resources. Turned out the public was more forgiving than she could have hoped. By the end of the week, it was mostly forgotten. Amazing.

But something Miller had said stayed with her. *Make people's lives a little worse.* He said they would accept it, that shared sacrifice, and even feel good about it. And Zuri could testify that was true. But then he tied that to the outages... and as she thought on it later, he didn't mean the ones he caused, not like Lucía had assumed at that moment. Gwen confirmed those had only been going on for a year.

Miller meant the normal outages. The ones that were planned and scheduled and had proper warnings. The ones everyone had woven into their lives. *It's just their reality.* But those outages were necessary... weren't they?

It had bothered her ever since he'd said it. The race to carbon zero had yet to be won. Every kilowatt had to be carefully managed. USEC kept building out power, but they hadn't made progress in moving past 80% renewables for the last five years. If Zuri had to say what ultimately made her place that call to the commissioner, the one she would tell everything and pray he wasn't a thread in Miller's carefully woven plot, it was that she had to know...

Was everything she believed about the grid a lie?

Stopping Miller would be enough. But that need to know the larger truth: that pushed her into taking the next step. Speaking of which... she shook off the reverie, checked her hair one last time, and then hustled on downstairs, slipped on her shoes, and scurried out the front door.

The sun was bright, and the morning warm—not the deadly heat of Palm Springs, but a balmy canyon day like any other. She strolled down the path with full awareness of all her blessings. She lived literally on top of a mountain, all her family gathered close, enough means to have all the things they could want in the world. She could shuck off the world's cares if she wished. But as her mother would say, they were born into this world with rights—rights they might have to fight for—but they were also born with obligations. And looking after those who couldn't do for themselves was one of them. A sacred one.

Zuri found her mother in her folding chair near the stage at the end of the clover park. Marcel and Denzel had hauled it out of the shed and set it up for Ruby. A small table to the side, under a pop-up awning, held the cookies and juice that would serve as refreshments after. Denzel had set up the folding chairs for their small family—two adult-sized and two peanut-sized ones—next to her mother's. Audre and Jayden were giggling with Ruby in the field behind the stage, trying to get her flower crown to sit on her hair, which someone had done up in adorably small Bantu knots. Granddaddy Terrell was settled in his chair, between the two Aunties. Denzel's client Michael had emerged from his cottage for the event, slumped awkwardly in a chair tucked next to the Aunties. Denzel and Marcel were chatting near the snacks. It was bustling and full of life, and she wished she hadn't spent a year running away from it. But life isn't convenient. It's what happens when you're struggling to get from here to there.

Zuri slid into the chair next to her mother.

"There you are." Her mother shielded her eyes against the sun to peer at Zuri. "Thought I'd have to come get you."

"Nope. I'm capable of getting here myself."

"That is a fact."

"I'm set to meet with Commissioner Sato on Monday," Zuri said. "Thanks for paving the way for that."

"Akemi is an absolute softy." Her mother shook her head, her trim silver afro decorated with golden butterflies for Ruby's debut. "And he has an inexplicable fondness for me. Never understood it."

"It's your great charm."

Her mother snorted then peered at her. "Is Lucía back to work already? She wants to bring some of Ellis's research papers up to the Hillstead this afternoon to discuss."

"I told you, she was back on Power Island One on Wednesday."

Her mother scowled. "Seems awfully fast after what happened."

"She's fine." Zuri smiled. "And happy. She gets to work the Island without Miller there. Or Astra."

"Well, thank heavens for that."

Zuri hesitated, torn between asking more about Ellis and just keeping it light. Ruby's performance was starting soon. "Does Lucía have any good theories? About Ellis's secret discovery?" Zuri and her mother had both worked in Ellis's lab, and Lucía was very enthusiastic about cracking the mystery of Ellis's discovery, but Monique was the true scientist among them.

"We'll see what she's dreamed up." Her mother looked at her sideways. "You're joining us, right?"

Zuri smiled. "Absolutely."

She gave a small nod like that's how it was supposed to be. And it was. "I don't know what Ellis has gotten up to, but if the CEO of Renew Energy is allowing his facility to be co-opted for this secret research, and DARPA is somehow involved, as you suspect, it has to be something big in scope. Something that would change the energy industry."

"Or weapons."

"Could be both." Her mother shrugged. "Physics is strange. Quantum Mechanics is downright bizarre. And I've never met anyone who understood the weirdness better than Ellis. Let's hope they don't burn down the world before Monday."

Zuri gave a small laugh, but it wasn't all that

funny. "Maybe I should get you to teach me SubGrid before the world ends."

Her mother lifted both eyebrows. "You hate that game."

"No, I hate *all* games. But this one, my mother likes."

She smiled and laid her hand on Zuri's and squeezed.

"Attention, everyone!" Denzel announced. While they'd been chatting, everyone had taken their seats, and he was up on the makeshift stage with an adorable but nervous-looking Ruby clutching a piece of paper.

Zuri caught her eye, smiled wide, and gave her a thumbs-up. Ruby gave her two thumbs-up in return then went back to fussing with her crown.

Denzel cleared his throat. "It is my great pleasure to announce Ms. Ruby Walker's debut performance on the Hillstead Hilltop Theatre. She will be reciting the poem *In This Place (An American Lyric)* by Amanda Gorman."

A vigorous round of applause went up as Denzel skipped down from the stage and landed in the chair next to Zuri. His hand found hers, and with one hand holding her husband's and the other holding her mother's, Zuri was more than ready for this. For all of it. Little Ruby's mother might not be here in anything but spirit, but Zuri beamed with all the pride she knew her sister would have at this moment.

As Ruby started, her voice was soft. Everyone hushed and strained to hear. As she got through the first stanza, her voice grew a little more confident, a little more loud. Gorman was one of the family's favorite poets. Her pieces made frequent appearances at the Hilltop Theatre. This was one of her early ones, back when she was just a young woman, not the towering figure of literature and politics she was today. Rumor was she'd finally decided it was time for that presidential run.

Ruby's voice lifted with each stanza, and she started to look up from the page. Each time, she found Zuri's wide smile waiting for her. Ruby mimicked Gorman's famous cadence and hand motions in her seven-year-old way. She was leaning into her stage performance. And the words were more powerful to Zuri's heart than if Gorman herself were speaking them. They were Amani's heart singing out from little Ruby's lips.

a history written that need not be repeated
a nation composed but not yet completed

. . .

Composed, but not yet completed. Her life. The country. Little Ruby's future. All of it was still to be written. All of it was theirs to determine. Their choices to make.

As Ruby rose through the rest of the piece, Zuri squeezed her husband's and mother's hands, holding herself back from cheering. When her niece finished and took her sweeping bow, everyone leapt to their feet and clapped and clapped.

Ruby popped off the stage and ran up to her.

Zuri gave everything she had to that hug. Her whole self.

Amani would have done nothing less.

The Nothing is Promised series continues with

Of Kindness and Kilowatts.

Download Book 3: Of Kindness and Kilowatts

Humanity is trapped in a loop.

As the world heats, it takes more energy to keep humanity from dying—a feedback loop that makes net-zero carbon increasingly impossible to reach.

Akemi's job on the Public Utilities Commission has its own daily disasters—making sure the infrastructure of civilization keeps running is the most thankless job on the planet. When a double event hits—heatwave plus viral breakout—keeping the power on is an all-out battle. It doesn't help that he's distracted by his elderly father, who was struck down and neuro-compromised by the same virus that killed his mother the year before. Now his father is living in Akemi's attic. They'd never had a relationship before, and that was a fair description of the state of things now.

Then an old friend's daughter shows up with a mystery of physics... and a tale of stolen kilowatts and deadly intrigue. He would dismiss it outright, except she's also the Regional Director of the power grid. Something isn't right, and the Governor won't accept excuses when the power goes out.

Sometimes, you're the right person in the right place, whether you want to be or not.

Of Kindness and Kilowatts is the third of four tightly-connected hopepunk novels in a near-future climate-fiction series. It's about our future, how the world is always more complicated than it seems, and how just when it seems like things couldn't possibly get worse, they invariably do... and that's when we discover kindness and quantum entanglement are what hold everything together.

———

Subscribe to Sue's Newsletter

to be the first to know about new releases:

http://smarturl.it/SKQsnewsletter

CHAPTER ONE

"There's a possible viral outbreak in Huntington Beach."

"How possible?"

"The WSO's going to announce a Level One

Airborne Alert this morning, with a bump to Level Two if it's not contained within 48 hours."

Akemi sighed. "Well, that's a pleasant start to the day." The World Science Organization's alerts were a vital, life-saving service, but this was a complication he didn't need today. Not that any day was good for WSO alerts.

Akemi's Chief of Staff and Legal Advisor gave a small smile. "I know you like the bad news first." Leo Ashton did know him. He'd advised Akemi for most of his ten years on Southern California's Public Utilities Commission. The man was only slightly older than Akemi's fifty-five years, but Leo's responsibilities at SC-PUC had already carved lines in his pale skin and whitened his hair with distinguished streaks.

"To be clear, I *don't* like bad news." Akemi adjusted his perch on the neutral-posture stool he'd recently swapped out for his chair and then, once balanced again, folded his arms. He'd already dialed down the window behind him to fifty percent for this morning's briefing, but the sun still warmed his back. "I'd just prefer to hear it from my advisors than to see it on the news. Do you have bad news for me as well, Martina?"

"Just the usual, Commissioner Sato." Ms. Enriquez, his Energy Advisor, was sitting at attention on the edge of her traditional office chair, which sat next to Leo's on the other side of Akemi's narrow, more modern desk. He'd recently replaced that too, donating the heavier, more ostentatious desk back to surplus for someone whose style it fit. He needed little table space —just enough to hold his tea, the framed picture of his family, and the kawaii character figure he was currently working on. Akemi may experiment with ergonomics and style for himself, but for his guests, especially his own advisors, comfort was far more important.

"Let's take care of this outbreak first, then." Akemi unfolded his arms to swipe the air and open the report Leo had just sent him. He quickly scanned the document's projected image as it hovered in the air, his chip automatically adjusting for the light from the window to make it easier to read. A stray thought flicked across his mental landscape, momentarily stealing his attention. The neural connections for his chip were standard. A base station clipped at his waist performed most of the processing while the chip implanted at his temple sent overlays to his optic, taste, and scent nerves via filaments delicately threaded through his brain. Implantation was safe and routine. But what if damage, perhaps caused by a virus, occurred in the brain long after implant? Could the neurological impact of an infection corrupt a standard chip's operation? Akemi tapped open a note and sketched the symbol for "mind" in Kanji—he only knew a few of the thousands of Japanese ideograms, but he was learning, and he'd memorized this one. He filed the note and pulled his attention back to the task at hand. "Level One Airborne Alert," he mused aloud to let Leo and Martina know he was working the problem. "I guess the people of Huntington Beach will be masking and enduring anti-viral sprays before they can visit their loved ones in the hospital." He quickly skimmed the report but didn't find what he wanted, so he swiped it away. "I'm assuming the virus has been identified."

"It's a subtype of Influenza A, H_3N_3," Leo said. "They've traced the cross-over to seals but suspect there might be an avian origin."

"A bad day for the seals as well, then." Akemi tapped up a map of the electric grid for the LA Basin, quickly enhancing the Huntington Beach area. Like most of the coast, the shoreline in this area was constantly eroding, the harbor having to be relocated every decade. Yet humanity refused to relinquish those beachside communities until the sea literally stole them away. Which naturally brought humans and marine life into constant contact.

Akemi lived inland for a reason. "Does the WSO have a handle on the spread?" he asked Leo. His Chief of Staff, who was a biologist as well as a talented lawyer, sent him a link that popped up the WSO's Infectious Disease map. It was a weather map for viruses, based on extensive serologic testing, coordinated worldwide. One of the many ways the WSO and its parent organization, the International Energy Consortium, managed the endless rolling pandemics the climate brought them every year. Sometimes, every month.

"The map shows it in a pretty limited area." Leo shrugged. "You know how that goes."

"You mean how we live in a very densely populated area with international travel? And that a new contagion can easily exist in places we're not measuring? Yes. I am painfully aware." Akemi felt the irritation in his voice like sandpaper across his forehead. He physically wiped the sensation away and had an immediate urge to apologize. While it was not, in fact, his job to understand the details of every viral outbreak or ancient pathogen arising from the planet, it was his job to ensure the basic utilities upon which civilization depended. Leo and Martina were exceptionally talented advisors, part of a substantial work-force at the PUC, all essential to that task. Akemi merely sat at the pinnacle of that organizational chart, appointed by the governor to keep that promise to the public... or be held accountable for failing.

There was no room for his personal agitation in such a position. He knew that when he took it, and it pained him that such a small irritation was throwing him off. He knew the reason. The source of his stress was not here, on the SC-PUC floor of the IEC building in Los Angeles. It was at his home in the Valley, and he needed to take greater pains to keep it there.

"I'm sorry, Leo. I shouldn't have snapped at you." Akemi adjusted in his seat once more, pulling up the report again and reading over it more slowly.

"I think it's the chair, Akemi."

Akemi flicked a look at Leo, and a crinkle around his eyes said he was joking. "I like the chair."

"You don't *seem* to like the chair," Martina offered.

"Et tu, Martina?"

"Just an observation, Commissioner." Ms. Enriquez was younger, and she kept a more formal tone most of the time, which Akemi allowed but would never insist upon. Her expertise lay in the electrical grid, having worked on the Power Islands then moved inland through various regulatory positions. She would probably one day have his job, which he would fully support.

Perhaps that day should come sooner than planned.

"You are both, no doubt, correct," Akemi said as he finished reading through the brief report. There were already deaths associated with this new outbreak. The WSO would do their usual diligence in containing it as best they could, and the PUC would support them, but the viruses were an implacable enemy. They always won if you counted every life a loss. Which Akemi did. He closed the report again. "And yet, I will continue to torture myself in attempting to balance on a chair specifically designed to not balance." He gave a short laugh, and it felt awkward. It had been some time since laughter felt genuine. "Back to our Level One Airborne Alert. Our main concern is, of course, ventilation. Everyone in the alert area will be turning on their fans and cranking up the mix of outside air, putting demand on the grid. MUU levels will get bumped with the alert, and again if we have a heat event, but we all know there will be overages." The

Maximum Utility Usage levels set the household, corporation, or public sector buildings' maximum usage covered by the Utility Tax, and those levels got bumped up automatically under certain conditions well known and publicized by the PUC. People were extremely well versed in their MUU status, but they still frequently had overages during unusual events, despite the price of additional kilowatts being rather steep. It was a guardrail, not an absolute. "I know we've got overages factored into the demand models. Is there any additional multiplier in the case of two simultaneous events?" He directed that question at Martina, given her expertise.

She frowned. "I'll double-check, but I don't think so."

To Leo, he asked, "Has USEC been informed of the alert?" The US Energy Consortium was the country's liaison to the IEC, and Leo was on the committee that coordinated between USEC and the SC-PUC.

"They're aware," Leo said. "They're a bit pinched with the recent outages. Apparently, that drained some of their storage."

Akemi lifted his eyebrows. The weekend's drama at home had so preoccupied him that he'd nearly forgotten last week's outages—which was astonishing, given the singular nature of the attack, coming from someone hacking the grid, not any natural failure or weather event. In his ten years as commissioner, he'd never seen a successful assault of that nature. USEC's IT department was legendary in its ability to safeguard the nation's grid. During his tenure, there'd only been one other kind of outage—a freak El Niño storm that had destroyed a whole sector of offshore wind turbines. They'd been able to borrow power from all the states up the coast, even into the Canadian grid, but it had been a trying time. This new hack was even more worrisome, despite USEC's assurances that they'd safeguarded against a repeat. He was still waiting to get the report in his folder about their remedial plans.

"As it happens," Akemi said, "I have the Greater Los Angeles Area Regional Director of USEC coming in for an appointment this morning. I'll check with her on their status. Do we need to authorize any emergency reserves for this possible double-event we're facing? You know I don't like to power up the gas turbines unless I have to."

"I don't think that will be necessary," Martina said. "Our buildout plans to meet peak summer demand this year are mostly ahead of schedule. We'll be able to easily handle the surge if it's contained to the Huntington Beach area, depending on how long it lasts and if we have a coincident heat event. But it is already mid-June—probabilities are high on fire threats and heat events. I've sent the latest forecasts to your folder."

Akemi tapped the air to signal his chip to bring it up. "I want us prepared for it to spread. And for the greater public reaction. Are the mayor and governor going to issue statements?"

"Still waiting to hear back from the governor's office," Leo said. "The Mayor of Huntington Beach will shortly issue an advisory to the hundred thousand residents of the city. Just the usual, to follow WSO recommendations."

Akemi brought up the map of the grid once again. "I expect a good fraction of residents of nearby cities to proactively go Level One once they see the WSO's alerts. We could easily see several million households, not to mention the industrial districts, putting Level One load on the grid. More, if it officially spreads and if the governor raises the profile by issuing a statement. Worst case, we could have the entire LA Basin dialing up their refresh mix in the middle of a heat event."

"If it spreads, the WSO should go to Level Two," Martina offered, a hopeful note in her voice.

And that *would* be better. Not from a bio-hazard standpoint, of course, but in terms of public utility usage. Level Two would shut down major gatherings, enact mandatory leave for work and school, and reduce public transit usage. All of that would reduce overall demand and shift much of the load to residences, where people often had banked storage that could be demand-managed if need be. Distributed power generation made it easier to handle the load, although the communications and transport loads would also shift.

"I don't want us to assume a Level Two Alert will get us out of the surge," Akemi said, quickly swiping up a meeting request for his Transport and Communications Advisors. Normally, he alternated days on briefings, but this alert scrambled those plans. It wasn't exactly an emergency—yet—but he wanted them prepared. He sent a meeting request to his Water Advisor as well just to keep things orderly.

"One problem I foresee," Martina said, drawing his attention back, "is these ongoing protests at Renew Energy in Palm Springs. We were counting on that buildout to come online by the end of the summer, but Renew says they can actually go live sooner. *If* it's approved. The Commission votes on Wednesday." She gave him an expectant look.

"My intent is to approve," Akemi said, "but I don't have a sense of the rest of the Commission on this. What's your feel from their advisors?" All the staff talked, as Akemi was not only aware but encouraged.

Martina looked to Leo—as Chief of Staff, he was usually more plugged into the politics. "Last I heard, there's a 3/2 split in favor of approval," Leo said. "Vazquez and Rogers leaning against. They have concerns about the residents of Palm Springs. I can dig deeper into that if you like."

"I would like that. If there's a real reason we should not approve, I want to know that ahead of Wednesday." Leo was making notes, so Akemi turned to Martina. "Assume our worst case. This escalates in the next day or two, just as a heat event strikes. How close are we to our max power generation? How much would we have to borrow from, say, Northern California and Oregon, and are they in any position to deliver? Also: what's USEC's risk assessment on this? I need that remediation report and details on the drain in their storage reserves. A hacker leaving us critically compromised right before a double event is just the kind of emergency I don't want to have to explain to the governor. Nor do I want this to be the first time on my watch we have to violate our emissions goals." That was always the last resort. Fossil fuels were expensive, they didn't store well, and turning on the generator took time. It wasn't like a battery farm you could just flip on. Not to mention that violating emissions targets had a terrible impact on consumer compliance and trust.

Martina was taking notes, scribbling in the air as well. "I'll have that to you by lunch."

"All right." Akemi rose from his stool, which rocked a little underneath him. "I know we have other prep for the Commission Voting Meeting on Wednesday, and I know you've both sent me a pile of reports to read, which I haven't. Let's meet back here with the rest of the team at noon to make sure we understand the situation. I want time to feel out the other commissioners before we get to Wednesday."

"Got it," Martina said, also rising while still taking her notes.

Leo had finished his and swiped it away as he rose. "You also have meetings this afternoon for the Firestead proceeding and that national subcommittee on emerging technologies. Do you want me to go in your place?"

Akemi was tempted. But committee work was important, and it was much better if he were there personally. "Let's see how the morning rolls out."

Leo nodded, and they all quickly bowed in parting.

Akemi sighed and began to prepare his morning tea. The tin of gyokuro was plain black, with no markings to indicate the green tea within. He scooped out two generous mounds. His hōhin handle-less teapot was designed for the lower temperature steeping that gyokuro required. His mother had brought the set back from Kyōto on one of her many visits, a small pot with tapered-lip cups made of white porcelain. Blue bamboo stalks curled delicately around the sides. He carried the pot with both hands, much like a large tea cup, to his executive bathroom, and filled it from the hot tap which was at the ideal temperature for gyokuro. The set had, of course, two cups when his mother had given it to him. They shared it every day, usually in the morning before he started his work. When the virus took her a year ago—the same virus that ravaged his father's mind, leaving him to survive her—Akemi packed away one cup in the attic. His children would one day discover it, when he was gone. Then they could re-unite them.

For now, he drank alone.

He walked with measured paces back to his desk, taking his time until the tea was ready to pour. He dialed the windows to 100% and sipped while gazing at the IEC building's wave-shaped reflection in the nearby windowed tower. The sun's ever-present shine was harsh this morning, less sparkle and more a blinding reminder of how it was slowly roasting the planet.

Maybe it was time for him to retire.

He was far too young, but then nothing in life was promised. His beautiful wife, Ichika, who gave him four amazing children, didn't live to see her 45th birthday. Ichika had worked the dying wards, the ones where comfort came only from the staff as the viruses claimed victim after victim. Then, one day, she was the patient. It was ten years ago, another event horizon in his life, a single moment when everything irrevocably changed. The first singular event of his life happened before he was born. His impending birth had driven his parents apart, his father running back to Japan to attend to his career, while his mother remained in LA. It was her choice, preferring single parenthood to giving up her own career simply because she had a child. At the tail end of the 20th Century, such things were still expected of women in the country of her birth. Instead, she raised Akemi in LA, repatriating to Japan only when he'd grown and started his own education and career. When the virus took Akemi's wife, his mother had returned, this time helping him raise his own children. Now, she was gone too, another event horizon, another loss in the war with the climate.

Akemi drew in a breath and drank the last flavor-filled sip of his tea, now gone cold. His father was sick. He needed care. Akemi had brought him from Japan to live with his family because it was no longer safe for him to ramble around that tiny house alone. The towering, conflicting responsibilities of work and home had never been so irreconcilable.

His position on the SC-PUC was important—vital, even, in the race to net zero, which all of humanity was desperate to win—but he wasn't so arrogant as to think saving the world couldn't go on without him. His father had abandoned his family to chase after the glory and status of his career. Akemi had always been determined *not* to be that kind of man. Somehow, he still found himself in this position of power and prestige, the kind his father would envy if it were based on technical expertise, not politics. Something always stood between them—abandonment, the gulf of years, and now disease. If it were Akemi's mother or Ichika or any of the children in need of his care and attention, Akemi wouldn't hesitate. He would step down and spend those precious hours with his family while he had them.

Instead, it was his father.

Akemi couldn't decide if this was retribution for some unknown karmic crime or the universe laughing at his life-long drive not to be anything like Dr. Dai Sato. He let that question drift to the back of his mind, unanswered and unanswerable, as he rinsed his tea cup and pot, drying and returning them to their places on his narrow table.

It was nearly time for his next appointment. He tapped open the Regional Director's file—Zuri Hill-Gray—and smiled when the young woman's image slid into his view. The resemblance to her mother was unmistakable. Monique Hill had been a trusted partner, a fellow physicist, during that long-ago time when they'd helped design and establish the original Energy Island. Zuri looked like the Monique of that time, the same deep brown skin stretched over sharp features, her dark eyes shining with intelligence.

A soft tone sounded, and the reception bot announced Zuri's arrival.

Akemi strode to greet her at the door.

He waved it open, then stepped back to bow, arms at his side, deep with respect. "Welcome, Ms. Hill-Gray. Thank you for meeting this morning."

"Thank you for accepting my request on such short notice, Commissioner Sato." Only as Zuri came up from her bow did Akemi notice a difference from her file photo. Her hair in the image was short-cropped, but standing before him, her hair had grown longer in a more natural twisted style.

"Please come in." Akemi ushered her in, his smile feeling real for once. "Please tell me your mother is doing well. We only spoke briefly last week. I'm afraid work has demanded all my attention lately."

"She's fine." Zuri stepped into his office, and the door automatically slid closed behind her. "She sends her warm regards."

Akemi bowed again, slightly this time, the smile lingering. "Please give her my apologies for never having time for that tea we keep promising to share."

"I'm sure she would enjoy that whenever it happens." Zuri's smile was strained. "I have an urgent matter to discuss, Commissioner Sato."

"Yes, of course." He gestured her toward the chair, but she just shook her head. They remained standing. "Last week's outages were quite dramatic," Akemi continued. "I look forward to discussing USEC's remediation plan."

"I've sent the report to your folder." Her eyes squinted a little from the window's full light.

"Please excuse the glare." He quickly dialed it down to 50%.

"I'm not here to discuss the report, Dr. Sato." The squint fell away, but her expression was still overly intense.

"That's not a title I often hear anymore." Akemi's internal alert system raised a notch.

"I brought this to you *because* of your expertise—not on the utilities commission, but your work from before. My mother tells me you're a physics genius."

"Your mother's words are more kind than reality would support."

"I sincerely hope that's not true." Zuri's hands found one another, wringing her anxiety. "You were a professor in the Energy Group at CalTech. You worked with my mother in setting up the original fusion labs on Energy Island, not to mention facilitating the conversion to USEC's network of Power Islands. And you were a founding member of the Power Engineering Institute, establishing the Department of Physics and Power."

Akemi frowned. "Do you have an urgent physics problem I can assist you with, Ms. Hill-Gray?" His alert system was fully activated now. Something was very off about this conversation, not to mention the panic widening Zuri's eyes.

"I know who hacked the grid," she said. "And it's one of us."

Akemi blinked, the sudden swerve taking him aback. "And by *us*, you mean—"

"Miller Zendek, former designer of Power Island One." Zuri was rushing out the words now. "And James Ellis. And various others—"

"*The* James Ellis?" Dr. Ellis was a Nobel laureate in physics who had pioneered several innovations in fusion research—

"*Yes.*" Zuri dipped her head and dropped her voice, although there was no one else to hear them. "He and Miller hacked the grid, but it was only to stop me from investigating them siphoning power for their secret energy research program. I don't know what they're doing, but they've already tried to kill a power engineer named Lucía Ramirez *and me* to keep us from finding out."

Akemi leaned slightly away, almost by reflex. "Those are very serious charges." Could his affection for Monique have blinded him to something being very amiss with her daughter? She was the LA Basin's Regional Director for USEC, a position requiring intelligence and no small amount of political savvy. Yet she was standing in his office spouting wild conspiracy theories about renowned professors stealing energy from the grid. *Hacking the grid.* Yet the hack, and the outages it caused, undeniably happened...

"I know it's insane." But the tension in Zuri's shoulders had dropped, almost like the hard part had been getting the words out, not convincing him they were rational. "I didn't believe it at first. But Miller essentially confessed to me... and then he tried to have me *killed.* I relented to his demands to keep quiet, Dr. Sato. I couldn't risk my family. And I didn't have the power to investigate this any further. *But you do.*" She held out her hand—in her palm lay a small drive. "This is everything we have. All our data, our latest theories, everything we've been able to cobble together without alerting Miller. My mother and I have been working with Lucía to unravel what we can, but none of us have your expertise in physics. Or the power to take this investigation further."

Akemi slowly reached for her proffered data trove. "This is... very unusual."

Zuri sighed. It almost seemed like relief, as if the data drive were a cursed talisman that she'd successfully transferred onto him. "I know. If this is as far as it goes, then Miller will get away with whatever he's doing in those labs. And he'll get away with the attempts on my life and Lucía's. If it were only that, I'd probably have let it go already—but it's not. Ellis is on to something. Something big. And I can't sleep at night knowing Miller Zendek has control of it. Nothing good will come from that."

Akemi nodded slowly, just in acknowledgment that he'd heard her. "I can't make any promises, Ms. Hill-Gray." None of this made any sense, but her eyes had shed the anxiety she'd walked in with. Maybe this was all she would require of him. "I *will* examine what you've brought me. Tell your mother I'll look into it. But I can't promise any formal investigations."

"I understand. Thank you." Zuri bowed with the words, and he automatically returned it. "You know how to find me. And I'll help any way I can. But whatever you do, please don't connect this back to me. Or Lucía. Miller already has a target on our backs."

That part was alarming, if even partially true. "I'll use the utmost discretion."

She bowed and thanked him again, then quickly retreated.

Akemi stared at the closed door. What in the

world had just landed in his lap? He had no idea what to make of Zuri's brief, fervent request. He would keep his promise to her, but whatever was on this drive would have to wait. He had meetings to attend, reports to read, and the impending crisis in Huntington Beach. Plus, the situation awaiting him at the end of the day, at home. He didn't have time to chase after some tangled conspiracy about secret energy projects.

And yet... he couldn't say he wasn't intrigued. Monique Hill had never been the kind of woman who would chase after nonsense. Even if they'd kept only loose contact over the years, their friendship from before had bloomed precisely because her groundedness and good humor were so appealing. If her daughter were slipping into the allure of some strange conspiracy theory, well... that was alarming given her position at USEC. The whole thing merited his attention based on that alone. And if there were some actual corruption in this, especially related to the hacking of the grid, then as commissioner, he had an obligation to root that out. The state—indeed, the country and the world—were perilously close to losing the race for net zero. There was no room for error, no tolerance for rogue elements endangering the power supply and destroying public confidence.

Akemi slipped the small drive into his pocket, settled into his neutral-posture chair, then swiped up the first of a dozen reports he needed to pore over, synthesize, and be ready to act on before his advisors returned at noon.

Zuri's mystery would have to wait.

———

Download Book 3: Of Kindness and Kilowatts

NOTHING IS PROMISED

Hopeful Climate Fiction

In a world beset with climate-driven plagues, power engineer Lucía Ramirez just wants a family to join...but she finds a mystery on Power Island One instead.

BOOK 1, BOOK 2, BOOK 3, BOOK 4

HALFWAY TO BETTER

Solarpunk Anthology

A collection of short stories, each exploring a near-future where we're struggling to survive the climate crisis and build a better world.

CLOSET FULL OF TIME

Black Mirror-esque Anthology

The thing the machines consume is *us*.

———

SINGULARITY

Hopepunk Sci-Fi

Eli is a legacy human, preserved for his genetic code, but he would give anything to ascend with the rest of humanity.

———

MINDJACK

YA Sci-Fi

When everyone reads minds, a secret is a dangerous thing to keep.

———

ROYALS OF DHARIA

Alt-India Steampunk Romance

The Third Daughter of the Queen must go undercover as the fiancé of a barbarian prince to find a weapon of war.

———

DEBT COLLECTOR

Cyberpunk

When your debts exceed your potential life earnings, debt collectors come take your life energy and give it to someone more "worthy."

————

FAERY SWAP

Middle Grade Fantasy

Finn becomes stuck the Otherworld when a runaway faery prince steals his body.

————

BRIGHT GREEN FUTURES: 2024

(Edited by Susan Kaye Quinn)

Solarpunk Anthology

A collection of short solarpunk stories from guests of the Bright Green Futures podcast.

Podcast: BrightGreenFutures.wtf

————

Most of SKQ's books are available in audiobook:

http://smarturl.it/SKQAudio

—————

Get a free box set of Singularity novellas when you subscribe to SKQ's newsletter:

http://smarturl.it/SKQsnewsletter

ABOUT THE AUTHOR

Susan Kaye Quinn is a rocket scientist turned speculative fiction author who now uses her PhD to invent cool stuff in books. Currently writing hopeful climate fiction and solarpunk, but her works include SciFi, YA, gritty cyberpunk, steampunk romance, and that one middle grade fantasy. Her best-selling novels and short stories have been optioned for Virtual Reality, translated into German and French, and featured in several anthologies.

www.susankayequinn.com